The Round and Other Cold Hard Facts

La ronde et autres faits divers

J. M. G. Le Clézio

The Round
& Other
Cold
Hard
Facts

Translated by C. Dickson

University of Nebraska Press : Lincoln and London

Original title: *La ronde et autres faits divers* ©
Éditions Gallimard, 1982
Translation © 2002 by the University of Nebraska
Press. All rights reserved
Manufactured in the United States of America ⊗
Design: Richard Eckersley

Library of Congress Cataloging in Pub-
lication Data
Le Clézio, J.-M. G. (Jean-Marie
Gustave), 1940–
[Ronde et autres faits divers. English]
The round and other cold hard facts =
La ronde et autres faits divers / J. M. G.
Le Clézio; translated by C. Dickson
p. cm.
ISBN 0-8032-2946-1 (cloth: alk. paper) –
ISBN 0-8032-8007-6 (pbk.: alk. paper)
I. Title: Ronde et autres faits divers.
II. Dickson, C. III. Title
PQ2672.E25 R6613 2002   2002018085

Contents

The Round and Other Cold Hard Facts

The Round

T HE TWO GIRLS decided to meet there, right where Liberty Street widens out to make a small square. They decided to meet at one o'clock because courses at the stenography school begin at two o'clock, and that left them all the time they needed. And so what – even if they were late, even if they did get expelled from school – what difference did it make? That's what Titi, the older of the two, said, and Martine shrugged her shoulders, just as she always did when she agreed with something but didn't want to say so. Martine is two years younger than Titi, which means she'll be seventeen in a month, even though she looks the same age. But she's a bit of a wimp, as they say, and she tries to conceal her shyness by putting on gloomy airs, by shrugging her shoulders over the smallest things, for instance.

At any rate, it wasn't Martine who thought it up. Maybe it wasn't Titi either, but it was she who spoke of it first. Martine didn't seem very surprised; she didn't voice any loud objections. She simply shrugged her shoulders, and that's how the two young girls had reached an agreement. Even so, there had been a bit of a discussion regarding the place. Martine wanted it to be done out of town – at Les Moulins – for instance, out where there weren't too many people around, but Titi said, on the contrary, it was better right downtown, where people were walking around, and she was so insistent about it that Martine finally shrugged her shoulders. In the end, right in town or out at Les Moulins, it was all the same, it was simply a matter of luck. That's what Martine thought, but she didn't feel it wise to say so to her friend.

All during lunch with her mother, Martine hardly thought about the meeting. When it did cross her mind, she was surprised to find that it really didn't matter to her. It must not have been the same at all for Titi. She'd been going over the whole thing for days now. She probably even talked about it, sitting on a bench beside her boyfriend, eating her sandwich. As a matter of fact, he was the one who had first suggested lending his moped to Martine because she didn't have one. But it's impossible to tell what he really thinks about it all. He has narrow little eyes that are completely impenetrable, even when he's furious or bored.

And yet, as she turned into Liberty Street, not far from the square, Martine suddenly felt her heart thumping wildly. It's a funny thing, a heart that's frightened; it goes "boom, boom, boom" so hard inside of your chest and your legs get all weak, as if you were going to collapse. Why is she frightened? She doesn't really know; her head is cool, her thoughts detached, even a little bored; but it's as if there's another person who's panicking deep within her. In any case, she purses her lips tightly together and breathes carefully so that the others won't know what she's going through inside. Titi and her boyfriend are there, straddling their mopeds. Martine doesn't like Titi's boyfriend and she keeps her distance so that she won't have to greet him with a kiss. With Titi, it's different; she and Martine are real friends, especially this past year, and everything has changed for Martine now that she has a friend. Now she's less afraid of boys, and it seems as if nothing can harm her since she has a friend. Titi isn't pretty, but she knows how to have a good laugh, and she has nice, gray-green eyes; of course her red hair is a bit wild, but it suits her well. She always protects Martine from boys. Since Martine is a pretty girl, she often has problems with boys, and Titi helps her out; sometimes she even kicks or punches them.

Maybe it was Titi's boyfriend who had thought it up first. It's hard to say because they've all more or less been wanting to try it for a long time now, but boys are always full of talk, and they never do much of anything. So Titi had said that we were going to show them, we wouldn't back down, they could all just hang it up, all the boys and girls in the gang, and that after this Martine would have nothing to be afraid of anymore. That's why Martine can feel her heart pounding so wildly in her rib cage, because this is a test, a trial. She hadn't thought of that before but suddenly, seeing Titi and the boy sitting there on their mopeds at the street corner, in the sunshine, smoking cigarettes, she understands that the world is waiting for something, that something has to happen. And yet, things on Liberty Street are quiet; there aren't many people on the street. The pigeons are strutting about in the sunshine on the curb and in the gutter, moving their heads mechanically. But it's as if a profound void has crept in from all sides, brimming with anxiety, shrilling in the ears, a threatening void looming over the seven-story buildings, over the balconies, behind all the windows, or in every parked car.

Martine is standing still; she can feel the chill of the void within her, deep down in the center of her chest, and the palms of her hands are growing slightly moist with sweat. Titi and the boy are looking at her squint-eyed from the sunlight. They're talking to her and she can't hear them. She's undoubtedly looking very pale and wide-eyed with trembling lips. Then all of a sudden, it's gone, and now she's talking, her voice a bit hoarse, without really knowing what she's saying.

"Okay. Well, ready? Ready now?"

The boy gets off his moped. He kisses Titi on the mouth, then he goes over to Martine, who abruptly shoves him away.

"Go on, leave her alone."

Titi jump-starts her moped with a roar and steers it over next to Martine. Then they take off together, revving the motors. They ride along on the sidewalk for a minute, then both go down into the street, staying side by side in the bus lane.

Now that she's off on the moped, Martine no longer feels the fear in her body. Maybe the vibrations of the moped, the smell and warmth of the gas fumes have filled up all the empty places in her. Martine really loves riding mopeds, especially on a day like today, when the sun is shining brightly and the air isn't chilly. She loves to slip through the automobiles, her face turned a bit sideways to avoid breathing in the wind, and go fast! Titi had been lucky; her brother gave her his moped; well, he didn't really give it to her; he was waiting until Titi got some money to pay him back. Titi's brother isn't like most other boys. He's all right; he knows what he wants; he doesn't spend all his time talking a lot of nonsense like the others do, just to show off. Martine doesn't really think about him, but just for a few seconds it's as if she were with him on the big Guzzi, hurdling along the empty street at top speed. She can feel the wind pressing heavily against her face, when she's holding onto the boy's body with both hands, and the thrill of the curves when the earth upturns, like in an airplane.

The two girls are riding along by the sidewalk. The sun is at its peak, blazing down, and despite the fresh air there is a sort of drowsiness hanging heavily over the asphalt streets and cement sidewalks. The shops are closed, their iron gratings pulled down, and that too accentuates the feeling of torpor. Even with the noise of the mopeds, at times Martine can hear the gurgling of television sets talking to themselves on the first floors of the buildings she passes. There is a man's voice and then music that echoes strangely in the drowsy street, as if in a cave.

Titi's out in front now, sitting up nice and straight on the seat of her moped. Her red hair is floating in the wind, and her aviator jacket is billowing out from her back. Martine is riding directly behind her, and as they drive by the display windows of the garages, she glimpses their silhouettes slipping along out of the corner of her eye, like the silhouettes of horsemen in the cowboy movies.

Then suddenly Martine can feel the fear again, and her throat goes dry. She's just realized that the street isn't really empty; it's as if everything were already set up ahead of time, and they're moving toward what is going to happen without being able to change their course. She's filled with such terrible anxiety that everything begins to swim before her eyes, as if she were going to be sick. She'd like to stop, lie down somewhere – anywhere, on the ground, up against the corner of a wall – with her knees pulled up into her stomach to hold in the thumping of her heart, which is sending waves through her entire body. Her moped slows down, weaving a bit on the pavement. Far out ahead of her, Titi keeps on going without looking back, sitting up nice and straight on the seat of her moped, with the sunlight sparkling in her red hair.

The worst thing of all is the people waiting. Martine doesn't know who nor where they are, but she knows they're there, on all sides, up and down the street, following with their ruthless eyes as the caval-cade of two mopeds rides past the sidewalk.

What are they waiting for? What do they want? Maybe they're on the rooftops of the white buildings, on the balconies, hiding behind the curtains in the windows? Maybe they're far away, sitting in some parked car and watching with binoculars? Martine sees all of this in the space of a few seconds as her machine slows down, weaving on the pavement near the intersection. But in a minute Titi is going to turn around, come back; she's going to say, "Well? Well? What's wrong? What are you stopping for?"

Martine closes her eyes, savoring those few seconds of red night in the long, cruel day. When she looks again, the street is even more de-serted and still whiter, with the great river of black asphalt melting in the sun. Martine purses her lips tightly, just as she'd done a little ear-lier, to hold in the fear. All of them out there, the ones that are watch-ing, the ones skulking behind their shutters, behind their cars – she hates them so much that her lips start trembling again, and her heart is pounding wildly. All of these impressions come and go so quickly that Martine's head is reeling, as if she'd had too much to drink and to smoke. Out of the corner of her eye, she can still see the faces waiting, watching – the dirty skulkers behind their curtains, behind their cars. Thick-faced men with sunken eyes, bloated men with vague smiles, and in their eyes that glimmer of desire, that cruel glimmer. Women, hard-featured women, looking at her with envy and contempt, with fear also; and then the faces of the girls from the stenography school, faces of boys looking round, coming up, leering. They're all there; Martine can feel their presence in the bar windows, in the far recesses of the empty, sun-swept street.

When she starts out again, she sees Titi pulled up at the bus stop near the next intersection. Titi is turned halfway around on the seat of her moped; her red hair is blowing across her face. She too is very pale, because fear is racking her insides and making a knot in her throat. It must be the blazing sun that's causing the fear, and the blank, cloudless sky above the seventh floors of all the new buildings. Martine brings her moped to a stop beside Titi, and they both sit there very still, throttle in hand, not saying a word. They don't talk to one another; they don't look at one another, but they know that the round is going to start now, and their hearts are beating very fast, not from anxiety any longer, but from impatience.

Liberty Street is empty and white, with the sun high at its peak, crushing the shadows, the deserted sidewalks, the buildings with their windows like blank eyes, the cars slipping slowly along. How can everything be so calm, so far away? Martine thinks of the motors of some mopeds that explode like a thunderclap, and for an instant she sees the street opening out, fleeing under the tires engulfing it, as the windows shatter into a thousand bits, strewing small triangles of glass over the pavement.

It's all because of her, just her; the woman in the blue suit is waiting for the bus, not looking at the girls, a bit as if she were sleeping. Her face is red because she's been walking in the sun, and the white blouse under her blue suit jacket clings to her skin. Her small eyes are set deeply in their sockets; they don't see anything, or just barely, furtively, down at the end of the street, where the bus should be coming from. A black leather handbag, set with a gilt clasp that gleams sharply in the light, dangles lightly from her right hand. Her shoes are black too, yawning somewhat under her body weight, worn on the inside.

Martine looks at the woman in the blue suit so insistently that she turns. But her tiny eyes are hidden in the shadow of her brow, and Martine can't find them. Why does she want to catch the woman's eye? Martine doesn't understand what's happening to her, what's bothering her, what both worries and irritates her at the same time. Perhaps it's because there is too much cruel, harsh light here, weighing down the woman's face, making her skin perspire, shining sharply off the gilt clasp of her handbag?

All of a sudden Martine races the engine, and the moped lunges forward on the pavement. She immediately feels the air on her face and the sluggishness disappears. She's going fast, with Titi close behind. The two mopeds speed noisily along the deserted street and are off. The woman in blue looks after them for an instant; she sees the mopeds make a turn two streets farther down, to the right. The whining sound of the motors is suddenly cut short.

Several blocks away, not far from the train station, the blue moving van is pulling slowly away, loaded with furniture and boxes. It's an old truck that sits up high on its wheels, painted an ugly color of blue, that successive drivers have brutalized for over a million miles, slamming on the brakes and grinding the gears into place. Ahead of the blue truck, the narrow street is crowded with parked cars. As he goes past the bars, the driver leans out but can see only dark shadows in the backs of the rooms. He feels tired and hungry, or maybe it's just the terribly harsh light bouncing off the asphalt. Screwing up his eyes, he frowns. The blue truck speeds along the narrow street, and its motor rumbles louder each time it passes a carriage gateway. Behind, on the flat bed of the truck, furniture creaks, objects bump together in packing boxes. The heavy smell of diesel fuel fills the cab and spills out into the air in a blue trail of smoke that lingers along the street. The old truck pitches and rolls over the bumps; it bowls along somewhat like an angry animal. Pigeons fly up before its hood. It goes across one street, another street, hardly slowing down at all; perhaps the million miles it's traveled through the streets of the city have given it the right-of-way.

Second, third, second. The gears grind, the motor hammers on, misfiring. The blue silhouette flies over the shop windows, like some mad animal.

Back there, on the curb, the woman in the blue suit is still waiting. She's just checked her watch for the third time, but the hands seem to be stuck insignificantly at one twenty-five. What is she thinking about? Her red face is impassive; the sunlight barely traces the shadows of her eye sockets, her nose, her chin. With the light shining directly into her face, she looks like a plaster statue standing so very still on the curb. Only the black leather of her handbag and shoes seems to be alive, flashing sharply in the hard light. At her feet, her shadow is all crumpled up like a dead skin cast off just behind her. Maybe she's not thinking about anything, not even about the no. 7 bus, which should surely be coming soon, which is running along somewhere past the empty sidewalks, which stops to pick up two youths on their way to high school, then, farther along, an old man in a gray suit. But her thoughts are stopped; they're waiting, just as she is, in silence. She's simply watching – sometimes a moped as it goes by, making that cranklike noise, sometimes an automobile slipping over the asphalt, with that warm sound of wet streets.

Everything is so slow, and yet there's something like flashes of lightning striking the earth, signals blazing out all over the whole city, crazy bursts of light. Everything is so calm, seems on the verge of sleep, and yet there is this rumor, these stifled cries, this violence.

Martine is riding out in front of Titi; she's speeding along through the empty streets, leaning the moped so far into the curves that the pedals scrape on the ground, throwing out showers of sparks. The warm air brings tears to her eyes, presses against her mouth and nostrils, and she must turn her head slightly sideways in order to breathe. Titi is following a few yards behind, her red hair pulled back in the wind; she too is feeling high, from the speed and the smell of gas fumes. The round takes them far across town, then brings them slowly back, street by street, toward the bus stop where the lady with the black bag is waiting. It's the circular motion that makes them feel high too. The motion that goes against the white buildings, against the cruel blinding light. The round that the mopeds make wears a path down into the indifferent ground, etches out a cry, and that is also why, in order to put an end to this dizzy spin, that the blue truck and the green bus are driving down the streets, so that the circle will be completed.

In the new buildings, behind the windows like so many lifeless eyes, are strangers who are barely alive, hidden by the membranes of their curtains, blinded by the pearly screens of their television sets. They don't see the cruel light or the sky; they don't hear the sharp cry of the mopeds that sounds something like a scream. Maybe they don't even know that these are their very own children that are riding along, making the round like this – their daughters, with wind-mussed hair and faces still sweet with childhood.

Inside the cells of their locked apartments, the adults don't know what goes on outside; they don't want to know who's going around in the empty streets, on the frenzied mopeds. How could they know about it? They're imprisoned in plaster and stone; cement has eaten into their flesh, clogged their arteries. On the gray television screen there are faces, landscapes, characters. The pictures light up, flicker off, make the blue glow dance on the motionless faces. Outside in the sunlight, there can only be room for dreams.

And so the round that the mopeds are making comes to an end here, on this wide Liberty Street. Now the mopeds are speeding along in a straight line, flinging all the buildings, the trees, the squares, the intersections swiftly behind them. The woman in the blue suit is alone on the curb, as if she were sleeping. The mopeds are running right along by the sidewalk, in the gutter. Martine's heart isn't beating wildly anymore. On the contrary, it's calm, and her legs don't feel weak now; her hands aren't sweating. The mopeds are both moving along at the same pace, right beside one another, and the sound of their motors is vibrating in such close unison that it could make the overpasses and the walls of the houses crumble. There are the men skulking in their stopped cars, hiding behind the curtains in their rooms. Let them go on spying with their narrow eyes; what difference does it make?

Almost without slowing, the first moped is up on the sidewalk, heading toward the woman in blue. When it happens and before she falls, the woman looks at Martine riding past her in the gutter; she finally looks at her, with her eyes wide open, showing the color of her irises, the light in her eyes. But that lasts only a fraction of a second, and then there is that scream echoing through the empty street, that pained and surprised scream, as the two mopeds flee toward the intersection.

Once again the warm wind is blowing, making your heart leap about in your rib cage, and Martine's hand grasping the black handbag is sweating. Above all, she feels a great emptiness deep inside of her, because now the round is finished, and she can't have that high feeling anymore. Far out in front, Titi is getting away, her red hair floating in the wind. Her moped is faster, and she makes it through the intersection; she's riding off. But just as the second moped is passing the intersection, the blue moving van comes out of a side street, just like an animal, and its hood catches the moped up and smashes it to the ground in a terrific crash of metal and glass. The tires screech as they brake.

Silence settles back down on the street, in the middle of the intersection. On the pavement, behind the blue truck, Martine's body is sprawled, flopped over on itself like a rag. There's no pain, not yet, as she lies there looking up at the sky, eyes wide, lips trembling slightly. Instead, an unbearably intense emptiness is slowly creeping over her as dark rivulets of blood trickle from her crushed legs. Lying on the pavement not far from her arm, as if someone had stupidly forgotten it there on the ground, is the black leather bag, with its gilt metal clasp glinting murderously.

Moloch

TODAY, August 15, 1963, the young woman named Liana is alone, sitting on the dark green, vinyl-upholstered wall sofa at the back of the front room. Outside the heat is beating down on the sheet metal walls, on the flat roof, and despite the open windows, there is not a breath of air. At Liana's feet, Nick is panting noisily. It is the only sound inside the trailer except for a motorcycle or a chain saw or the peculiar sounding shout of a child from time to time off in the distance that makes the young woman shudder. It's as if there's no one, absolutely no one, for miles around because the silence is weighing down as heavily as the heat; it is suffocating; it is like a vice on your head; it prevents you from thinking.

It's been so long since Liana has seen anyone. The last time was ... two, maybe three days ago? Liana can't really remember; she can barely get her mind to concentrate on digging up memories. When she tries, something clicks inside of her, like a small muscle growing tense, like the little nerves that start twitching in your eyelid or in your cheek. It's a signal for her to stop searching. So she gets up and walks a little way down the length of the mobile home, barefoot on the old nubby carpet marred with cigarette burns. The floor of the mobile home shakes under her feet. The wolf dog looks up, pricks his ears forward. Then he drops his head again and goes back to sleep or pretends to go back to sleep. He hasn't seen anyone for days either, but he probably doesn't care. He doesn't like anyone, doesn't need anyone.

His name is Nick. She's not the one who picked the name. It was Simon, when he brought the dog over. He had simply said, "His name is Nick." He was still so young that he could hardly stand up, and he always peed right underneath himself on the carpet. Liana was fond of him all the same; she would have liked to give him a nice, sweet little name, but Simon had said his name was Nick; that was all. So she accepted the name, and it was rather fitting for a wolf dog. When Liana looks at Nick, nothing clicks in her, and she can conjure up the old days without it being painful. But she has to think only of the dog, nothing else; if not, there's that dizziness, like a whirlwind in her head, a draining wind that paralyzes her.

Nick is a big wolf dog with a gray and white coat, a black furry collar, and a dark gray tail. He has tiny white socks at the tips of his paws; something like a beauty mark on each side of his face; long, stiff whiskers; and a black patch above each eye. He has yellow irises set off with very black pupils that stare straight into your eyes till you have to look away. Liana is trying to imagine the dog's eyes right now, and though she doesn't realize it immediately, it is Simon's eyes that appear – yellow eyes too, hard and insistent, with that little gleam of light that shines in the center of his pupils, making them even blacker. The eyes look at her for a long time, and the silence inside the mobile home is so intense that dizziness hollows out its deep well, unbearable. Why are those eyes staring at her like that, for such a long time? She thinks they are trying to see inside of her, bore down to the very quick, burn her up, kill her. She feels the two black shafts of those eyes piercing through her, and she cries out.

The wolf dog has lifted his head again, he looks at her with half of his body ready to spring. Then since she doesn't say anything, doesn't move, he feels reassured and gradually relaxes his muscles. But he doesn't lay his head back down on the rug between his paws. His yellow eyes remain wide open.

"It's nothing, Nick, it's nothing," says Liana. She notices that she hardly has the strength to murmur those words and that it's not really true because her whole body is trembling and sweat has broken out on her forehead, her back, and the palms of her hands.

What time is it? One o'clock, maybe later? If the television still worked, she could see if the news was over yet. But the set broke down last week; it suddenly started fuming, giving off a choking black smoke.

Yet it certainly isn't later than one o'clock because the highway out there at the other end of the vacant lot hasn't started its noise up again. When it's nearing two o'clock, you can hear motors rumbling, especially the semis. They're still stopped in front of the cafés and gas stations on the outskirts of the city. They're eating; everyone's eating. Suddenly Liana thinks that she's hardly eaten anything since last night. She'd gotten hungry a little while ago and then it passed. That's the way it always is nowadays, ever since... She gets hungry and then the next minute she feels nauseous. Maybe it's because of the baby? Maybe she should go and see a doctor, like that pale young woman with glasses, a social worker, says. But she doesn't like doctors. They always want to touch you, examine you, they're always prying... If she goes to see a doctor, he'll surely ask her questions, and his eyes will be all shiny. People so love to pose questions. They have shiny eyes and they talk with wet lips, saying things, asking about things, wanting to know names.

Nick doesn't talk. He doesn't ask any questions. He knows how to remain motionless for hours, days, simply watching and listening, without making a sound.

Silence is everywhere. Liana can feel the silence within her, an endless silence. Outside in the torrid heat, in the light, the trees aren't moving. They are scrawny trees with dull leaves, eucalyptuses, laurels, some pines, palms. The earth is white, stones and dust. But Liana doesn't need to look outside. The silence that is everywhere is also within her, and her eyes sweep the horizon like a searchlight that sees all.

She hasn't gone out for so long now. Two, three days? In the sweltering mobile home there's nothing to stop time, nothing that keeps the hours, the minutes from passing. The electric clock is stopped; the battery probably went dead, but Liana doesn't even consider replacing it. What use would it be? She wouldn't even know how to set the time, and what does she care about time anyway? She simply watches the light changing color inside the mobile home. In the morning, the light is pale and fair, a little gray. Then when the heat rises outside, it turns a brutal, painful yellow, and Liana squints her eyes to look at it. Afterward comes the warm, slanting light in which you can see motes of dust hovering like gnats. Still later there's the soft orange light, the very peaceful, spent light of the declining day that slowly changes into dusk's purple veil. Then it becomes gray, but not the same gray as in the morning: a gray that gradually dies away, ash-colored. Even when the sky is completely dark, light still filters into the mobile home; it comes from the dreary glow of the streetlamps out there on the highway and the pinkish haze of the city lights. Every once in a while the beams of an automobile go slipping by. You can spend hours watching the light glide over the walls in the mobile home and the reflections hurrying across the green vinyl of the sofa, over the varnished table and the flowered pattern of the curtains.

Liana moves as little as possible. She is heavy, very heavy. Sometimes when she walks, her knees give way and she nearly falls down. It's as if she had someone sitting on her shoulders. Sometimes she thinks of Simon; she can feel the weight of his body on hers, and she shakes herself in rage to make him fall off. But the unknown weight doesn't go away; it never leaves her.

So she prefers not to move. She just sits there, sometimes on the wall sofa near the window, sometimes on a chair, with her elbows leaning on the table.

Where could she go? Everywhere, here and elsewhere too, is the same chalky earth, the sand, the sharp rocks, the glaring, acrid earth. Everywhere, those scrawny trees, those eucalyptuses, those laurels, those sun-worn palms. There are plane trees along the roads and aloes on the banks of the river. True, they don't move. The trees and the aloes stay right where they were born, trapped in the parched earth, scorched in the sun.

But the others, the people. They would know how to find her quickly; she couldn't escape them. The men and women who move around constantly, who come and go in their automobiles, bikers with helmets out there on all the roads, and trucks on the highways. They all know where they're going; they're not afraid of getting lost; they don't waste any time. Liana knows they might come any minute, take her away, haul her off to their prisons. They're looking for her every day – the doctors, the policemen, the social workers, the ambulance drivers. Liana is afraid of them, of the noise they make, of their haste. They run the streets endlessly on their machines; the sound of all their motors mingles together and roars over the city like the sound of a cataract.

Every so often she walks a little way down the length of the mobile home. She can feel the metal chassis shaking under her feet, and the mobile home sways a little like a boat. Nick has lifted his head again, and he's watching his mistress with his yellow insistent eyes. Then he yawns and goes over to the door. He wants to go out.

Liana comes over to him.

"Do you want to go out?"

She puts her hand on the doorknob. Nick looks at her hand impatiently and lets out a little yelp, whimpering. Liana turns around, looks about for the leash but doesn't see it. Maybe it slipped down behind a piece of furniture. Liana is tired; she doesn't feel like looking for it. Maybe she lost it when she went to the supermarket with Nick the other day? She can't recall if Nick was wearing his leash when she came back. Oh well. She opens the door and Nick slips out. He trots quickly over to the middle of the white plain, just like a wolf. Liana knows that he's going off to hunt by the dry riverbed, that he'll kill some chickens, some rabbits, in the neighboring farms, but she doesn't care. It's like a pact between Nick and her. Maybe he'll come back at nightfall, exhausted, eyes shining.

Liana lets herself heavily down from the front step. She teeters on the hot surface of the earth. The light is blinding. She has to raise her right hand to screen her eyes. She walks straight out into the middle of the vacant lot. All of a sudden she realizes she's barefoot because the sharp stones are cutting her feet.

She tries to catch sight of the dog, but he has vanished onto the white plateau out beyond the hedge of scrub. She can hear the farmers' dogs barking as he passes.

Liana stands there in front of the mobile home without moving, and the light envelops her, penetrates her. She is all alone on the dusty earth, far from the trees, the houses, with nothing to lean against, to shelter her. The sun beats down in the center of the sky, throbbing out in painful waves. There are rings swimming before her eyes, and off in the distance there are fleeting silhouettes, shadows, maybe children or dogs or cars; it's hard to tell. There are swarms of invisible insects thickening the air, wasps, june bugs. Light is whirling about her like the wind, the light of silence, loneliness weighing down upon her like the heavy body of a stranger.

Liana would like to take a few steps backward but she staggers, and now it is the flat surface of the entire earth that begins to turn, pulling in its path the trees and the elongated metal bodies of the mobile homes, the electric poles, the scrub, the thin palms, the drums of kerosene, even the towering buildings on the banks of the large, dry riverbed and the supermarket with its corrugated iron roof.

It spins slowly, as if there were music playing somewhere. And suddenly Liana feels that she is falling; her body hits the ground like a piece of wood. Liana hears a loud noise in her head; then she doesn't hear anything more because she has fainted.

When she wakes up, she first sees two insistent eyes staring at her, with very black pupils. But they're not the dog's eyes. It's a young woman with a childlike face, wearing glasses that gleam sharply in the sun. Liana recognizes her immediately: it's the social worker, the one that often comes to talk with her at the door.

"Are you all right? Will you be all right now?"

The soft voice is also insistent. Liana slowly lifts herself up, like the dog did a little while ago. Her hair is full of dust. She instinctively combs through it with the fingers of her right hand. The young woman with gold-rimmed glasses is looking at her anxiously; she says:

"I'm going to get a doctor."

"No! No!" replies Liana sharply. "I'm fine; I'm going inside."

"I'll help you."

Liana tries to get to her feet on her own, but she's too heavy. She leans on the social worker's arm and limps over to the steps of the mobile home.

"Are you sure you don't want me to call a doctor?"

In a sort of rage, Liana says hurriedly, "No! I don't want to see anyone!"

"In your condition, it might be best, in case you have another dizzy spell."

The young woman has an insistent voice that Liana hates.

Liana says coldly, almost cruelly, "I don't have dizzy spells. My dog knocked me down."

And to make it seem truer she calls out two or three times like this: "Nick! Nicky! Nick! . . ." But of course the dog doesn't come.

She goes back toward the mobile home very slowly, taking each step with great care. All around her the light is blistering hot; sparks burst forth from everything, from the leaves, from the long gray fronds of the palms, the iron posts, the sharp stones. There are even sparks in Liana's hair, at the end of each of her nails. There's a sort of electrical storm passing over the vacant lot. It is making a strange kind of music too, a low, humming sound, a grating sound that gets inside of your ears and makes a knot deep down in your body. Liana feels her throat tightening with nausea. A cold chill makes the palms of her hands sweat, and her heart starts racing in her arteries.

"Are you all right? Are you all right?"

The young woman with the glasses is still by her side. She takes her arm above the elbow, and Liana lets her do it; she's too weak to resist. When they get to the front step, Liana wants to stop, but the young woman's hand guides her to the door. They enter the stifling heat in the trailer together.

"It's too hot in here," says the young woman. "Isn't there any air conditioning?"

Liana shakes her head.

"You should keep the door and all the windows open."

"No! No!" shouts Liana. She's half lying on the vinyl sofa.

"I'll get you something to drink," says the young woman. "You're probably suffering from dehydration."

She goes into the kitchen, and Liana hears her rummaging around in the clutter of dishes. Then she comes back carrying a glass of water. "It's not cold, but it will do you some good anyway."

Liana takes a drink. The water makes her feel less nauseous, and her heart is not beating so fast now. She's sleepy.

"Thank you," she says. The young woman looks at her very intently.

"You don't want me to open the other windows? It's really terribly hot in here."

"No!" says Liana. "It's . . . it's because of the flies."

"Flies?"

"Yes, the smell of the dog, it draws flies."

Liana glances around the mobile home. The young woman understands immediately.

"Don't get up. I'll call him. What's his name?"

"Nick."

Liana watches the young woman open the door. She calls the dog. That voice and the dog's name ring out oddly in the thick silence of the vacant lot.

The young woman comes back.

"He's not there. Do you want me to go looking for him?"

Liana shakes her head.

"There's no use in that. He'll come back in a little while. He'll be back before nightfall."

Since there's nothing else she can do, the young woman just stands there in front of Liana. Her childlike face is twisted with worry, with exhaustion, as if she were going to start crying.

"Is there really nothing I can do for you?"

Liana shakes her head.

The young woman is going to leave. But she changes her mind. She takes a notebook out of her bag, writes something on a piece of paper, tears it off, and hands it to Liana.

"It's my name and address and my phone number. If you need anything whatsoever, you can reach me there or leave a message. For Judith is enough. Will you remember that? Judith."

Liana looks at her without a smile, expressionless.

"Everything will be fine now; you'll see."

"I don't need anything."

"Goodbye."

"Goodbye, Ma'am."

"When you . . . when you go to the hospital, call me. I'll come and pick you up."

The social worker goes out and closes the door quietly.

Outside somewhere, the big black and white wolf dog is running at full speed over the dusty ground, through the scrub, along the dry riverbed. He's not listening to the sound of the automobiles as they roll past on the highway perched up on the concrete pilings. He's not listening to the strident chirp of the crickets or the children shouting in the fields. The light glints on the sharp stones, on the leaves, on the fronds of the palms, on the spikes of barbed wire. It's a light that is inebriating, that drives you a little mad. The large dog runs in large circles about the farms; he's following a very old track, and the dogs in the neighborhood start barking. Then he stops running at nightfall; the hair on his back bristles as he slinks on his belly toward the chicken coop fenced with wire mesh and slowly chooses his prey.

~

Today, October 3, Liana awoke before dawn. When she felt her water breaking, she realized that it was time, it was coming. She hadn't really thought about it yet and since she had stopped counting the days on the calendar long ago, she had sort of forgotten that it had to come some day.

She had been bloated and heavy for such a long time, the skin of her belly stretched tight like a watermelon. Maybe she'd gotten used to it all; it was her new mode of existence and it shouldn't change. She had simply grown a little more bloated and a little heavier each day; she got a little more winded when she walked, when she went up stairs and, near the end, even when she stepped up on the sidewalk. And then people started looking at her embarrassedly; you would have thought that somehow they had something to do with her predicament. There were even certain people that were kind to her, but overly kind, a little shifty-eyed, and Liana didn't trust them. When the young woman with gold-rimmed glasses came back, Liana cracked open the door each time and said to her meanly, as if to a person selling soap from door to door, "I don't need anything, thank you Ma'am."

Lately she even recognized the way the woman knocked at the door, very lightly, with just the tips of her fingers, and she didn't get up. The dog barked like mad until the social worker left.

Even so, she was a little scared now, feeling her water seeping out into the bed underneath her. She got to her feet to clean up and was suddenly overcome with strong contractions. Never had she felt such pain before. It was waves of fire surging down from her lower back, paralyzing her legs, then flowing back up to her shoulders, out to her arms, throbbing in her neck.

She fell to the dirty carpet, whimpering, unable to walk. She started breathing heavily, making a chugging noise like a machine, and she could feel every vein strung tight as a cord and her heart beating heavily, as though it were at the very core of the mobile home, shaking the sheet metal walls, the furniture, the floor.

Nick came toward her with his ears pricked up; his yellow eyes shone strangely in the glare of the electric light bulb. Maybe he knew what was happening. Liana called him silently with her eyes, clenching her teeth to keep from moaning. But he stopped some distance from the young woman and lay down on his belly, with his paws nice and flat on the carpet, his ears cocked, without taking his yellow eyes with their pinhole pupils from her.

Lying on the rug, Liana rolled over a little on one side, and despite the terrible pains that kept her from thinking or moving, she felt somewhat reassured seeing Nick there, as if he could really help her.

She didn't talk to him. She just lay there on the rug with her knees drawn slightly up toward her belly, hugging her arms around herself and moaning softly, pursing her lips tight to keep from screaming. The moaning welled up from within, surging along the length of her whole body with the violent waves of pain that crashed up against her closed lips and then fused into contained vapor. She was moaning for herself and for Nick too; she was trying to transform the pain into a droning song that might help her to fall asleep, to forget.

But Liana can't go to sleep. The waves of pain are coursing through her body, coming from very far away, from out on the other side of the world; along the way they run up against the shell of the mobile home and inside the shell, the woman lying on the carpet, curled up, trying in vain to hide. There is so much suffering on earth! The ashen earth, the trees, the palms standing stock still, the gray night, the lampposts and their sickly light, and all the rest, those sheets of metal, those windowpanes, those plastic surfaces, those vinyl upholstered cushions. And him, the big black and white wolf dog, lying on his belly like a stone statue, hieratical; and outside, the women, the men, strangers who sleep intertwined amid mussed sheets, who are alone; sick people in long hospital rooms, old people who are suffocating, all of them out there in their stuffy, airless rooms. The loneliness is so vast it is filling up the whole inside of the mobile home. It is flooding in, coming from the darkest depths of the night in waves that grow closer and closer together and ripple over the pale blue stars of the streetlamps, spreading its terrifying silence, and the moaning of the woman's voice is like the buzzing of a mosquito.

The big dog lying near her doesn't move. He watches her with his yellow eyes, listens. Liana would like to call him; she thinks of his name and the other name too, the one that is pronounced Simon, and this time she's not overcome with dizziness. Liana doesn't want to scream, she can't. She doesn't know why, but she mustn't scream; no matter what happens, she mustn't. So she pinches her lips even more tightly closed over the pain, and her opened knees allow her arms to hug her large hard belly, holding it in like a belt.

Slowly, instinctively, her arms begin to make a kneading motion, their work of expulsion. They slide down either side of her belly, hands clasped tightly, then move back up to her breasts, slide back down again, and again. It is their way of struggling against the waves of pain, warding them off, countering their offensive. Liana turns over on her back, then lets her body fall alternately to the left, to the right, and the rolling movement feels good. She's like a boat rocking on the waves, drawing back for an instant and then tipping up dangerously as the powerful swell slips under its hull.

The moaning is rolling too. Sometimes high pitched, powerful, when the wave lifts, making the whole frame crack, shaking everything in its wake; sometimes soft and deep, slow motion, and her heart and lungs slow down too, and time in the world slows down, like a soft breath.

It lasts a long time, such a long time that Liana can't remember how it all began. At times she thinks that the baby is being born, that that's what it is, what she's been awaiting for months now, that something extraordinary is happening for the first time, something that will change the entire world. It makes her whole body jolt and tingle, like an electrical shock burning and lighting everything up inside, like a fiery tongue of alcohol running through her.

But that doesn't last long because of the suffering, because of the loneliness from the depths of night tightening around the hull of the mobile home. All that remains is pain, the desperate, breathless pain that comes from every corner of the dry earth, from the waterless bed of the river or from the sleepy city haze. That comes through the shadowy halls of the never-ending night and spreads, forks into the bristling branches of the trees, into the bitter leaves of the old aloes.

The wolf dog is not moving. His yellow eyes watch the young woman fixedly as she rolls slightly from side to side, lying on the green carpet, her dress thrown up around her bloated belly. His eyes are hard; his ears twitch imperceptibly, just to listen to the creaking of the floor under the woman's body, the continuous waves of moaning.

Maybe he is commanding all of the pain. Maybe it is in his eyes, which are so hard, so yellow; which seem to stem from another world, from out there, from the very source of heat and light, from memory's scorched shores; which are born of the same light as the seed of the man that was left in the woman's belly; so the seed grew, causing its explosions of pain, wrenching open, spreading wide, forcing the flesh that resists it, throwing out long, feverish chills through her limbs, thrusting its waves through her entrails all the way into her lungs, her heart.

Just before daybreak, the child is born. Liana hadn't noticed it was coming. She simply realized she couldn't get up, couldn't walk away or even call for help. It was too late. Her feet thrust her body up into an arch as if she were doing a backbend; the movement was so powerful that Liana thought she would push back the narrow walls of the mobile home and even the land outside, the trees, the electric towers, the dense night. Then the baby slowly appeared, first its head slipping gently out, and Liana's hands guided it into the world. Liana looked at the ceiling of the mobile home, the bare electric light bulb that shone out as brightly as a star. Her hands were doing all the work, and her belly too, dilating and contracting regularly. The hands guided the child between her opened legs; they laid it on the carpet, all sticky and still covered with the membranes of the placenta. The hands also broke the umbilical cord and tied it around the baby's middle. Already the sharp wailing filled the mobile home, and the light of day began to pale the glare of the electric light bulb.

Then Liana suddenly felt as though she'd been liberated from her anxiety, for the first time in months, without really understanding why. Maybe it was simply that this new life filled everything up inside the hull of the mobile home and there was no more room for anything else. It was so hot that Liana didn't wrap the little girl up. Instead, without rising from the bloodstained carpet, it was she who undressed completely. Then she brought the tiny being to her breast, hugged it against her swollen bosom. She went to sleep like that, lying on her side on the floor with the baby in her arms, as the broadening daylight flushed over the windows of the mobile home.

～

The wolf dog with the yellow eyes is watching intently. Not a thing on his body or in his eyes is moving. His black and white coat shimmers in the sunlight, each sparkle of light as hard and compact as a gemstone. There is no rest on earth, nor any gentleness, ever. The sunlight is dry and harsh; it comes from the vast empty spaces, from the dusty shores of gravel at the mouth of the great river.

Time is so drawn out here in the metal hull of the mobile home; it's as if everything were stopped, baked hard in the dry heat, petrified, bombarded by the myriad of electrical sparks. Just like the stones, like the bits of flint sunk into the powdery earth, like the twigs on the charred bushes, the trees withered with thirst, the gray leaves of the aloes, the palm fronds hanging in the heavy air, up in the sky. The wolf dog fixes his yellow eyes with pinpoint pupils straight ahead, without moving. There is strength in his gaze, in his muzzle, in the vertical furrows of his brow. The strength also comes from the long, straight hairs sticking out of the small black patches over his eyes and from his whiskers, short and brittle, with some of the hairs broken off. The strength comes from his chest, from his front paws stretched out before him, with the claws dug into the dirty green carpeting of the mobile home.

He's not moving. It is his will to remain motionless, his strength. It's like a command that he doesn't understand but that he hears. A command that has gripped his whole body, that has strung every nerve, every muscle taut. Maybe it came from the blinding noon sun, when Liana opened the door of the mobile home and left. It was then that a painful sort of wave had pushed him all the way to the back of the mobile home, and the hard voice of his mistress, a voice he'd never heard before, had shouted the order only once.

The yellow eyes of the dog are watching the sofa near the window. They remain riveted on the green, vinyl-covered cushions and the towel spread out on them because the small child is sleeping on the unfolded towel. She's not moving either; she barely makes faint little sounds when she breathes because the air is too hot and weighs on her chest. But she sleeps without moving, lying on her back with her head turned to one side and her fists closed tight.

The wolf dog stares at her. He's keeping a very close watch on the child with his yellow eyes because she is the only living being on earth, the only one who has a heart, a face, a pair of hands.

Maybe it's because of the smell. The wolf dog has smelled nothing but her for days now, an odd odor that he'd never smelled before, a bit sweet and stale, a strange mixture of sweat and urine, but pleasant, very pleasant, something like the smell of a plant or a flower. Because of that smell, the wolf dog can't sleep. At times, his eyes droop closed; he lays his jaw on his two front paws and he lets himself drift toward sleep. Then all of a sudden the smell hits him. It alerts him; it slips inside of him and makes his ears stand up and his eyes open wide, and every nerve in his body draws up taut as a bowstring.

The smell of the small child is very sweet; it fills the inside of the mobile home. Maybe it has even spread outside, over the vacant lot, into the trees, all the way out to the pilings under the highway and over the deserted beaches of the great dry river.

The wolf dog likes the smell. He doesn't really know that he likes it, but every fiber in his body is tense, painfully tense, straining to better take in the smell. It makes him restless – the frail unbroken sound, the faint fluttering heart, the tepid, fleeting breath, the blood running through the veins, pulsing under the delicate skin.

He listens, sharp-eyed. Without moving, his powerful paws

stretched out in front of him, he listens. But it's like his gaze, his sharp ears pricked up, straining, painful. Little noises creep in from outside – cracking noises, breaths of wind, shrill sounds of insects. Sometimes, off in the distance, distorted by the heat, sounding unreal, the shouts of children, the barking of dogs come floating over. Or sometimes the rumbling of trucks as they lumber up the viaduct on the highway. The sounds are mingled with the light, with the heat, with the loneliness. They reach the wolf dog's ears, but he doesn't budge; they echo out at the very same time that he imagines them. But his ears are raised and turned forward, hearing only the faint sound that comes from the vinyl-upholstered sofa.

The baby is breathing softly, a bit laboriously due to the heat. The even sound of her breathing fills the metal hull of the mobile home. It seems as if something springs from her breathing; maybe the heat and the light are coming from it; the stale smell that keeps the dog from sleeping is coming from it.

When the baby awakens and begins to cry, Nick doesn't move. But his eyes grow harder; his whole body becomes extremely tense. His nails dig down further into the carpet, and the hair on his back and shoulders bristles slightly.

Emptiness has reigned in the mobile home for so long, for hours, ever since Liana closed the door and walked off across the vacant lot. And the emptiness is elsewhere too; it's out on the stretches of dusty earth, in the groves of sun-scorched trees, on the leaves of the laurels and eucalyptuses, in the white bed of the river. Everything has been echoing through his body, pounding on the metal and glass walls for such a long time. Now the cries of the small child fill the entire mobile home. They tumble out shrill and sustained, insistent like the song of insects. The child is crying out against the silence, against the loneliness, boring a hole into the thick air, the thick metal walls, a hole through which the silence can escape. There is no one else here in the mobile home, no one but the high-pitched cries and the steady gaze of the wolf dog.

Suddenly Nick feels hungry. He hasn't eaten in so long. His mouth and his tongue have become numb, and he can't even recall what they used to feel like. Hour after hour, without really looking at it, he's been keeping watch on the door of the mobile home, waiting for Liana to come back, waiting for her to appear in silhouette against the light, for her to speak to him, call him. For days now he's been waiting for her to feed him – anything, some meat, cookies, bread. But Liana didn't look at him anymore when she walked into the mobile home. She went straight to the sofa, lay down on the cushions, and unbuttoned her dress, and the small being sucked voraciously as she pressed it to her breast. Then came the smell of milk and sweat that spread through the mobile home, penetrating everything. That odor was painful for Nick; it frightened him a little too, and he went and hid under the table at the other end of the metal hull, with his eyes squinting and his ears lying back.

Now the sweet, stale smell of milk, urine, and sweat is filling the mobile home, but Nick isn't afraid now. The baby's body is growing larger, filling up all the space with its warm skin, its face, its breath, its cries.

The baby is crying harder now. Maybe she's noticed that her mother is gone, or maybe she too is hungry. But her hunger is small and gentle; she wants to suck at her mother's warm breast, fill her mouth with thick milk; she wants to be enveloped in the warmth of the body she loves.

Nick's hunger is different; it's a hunger that he doesn't recognize anymore, a hunger nothing can satisfy. His hunger is like the loneliness at the mouth of the dry river, where the dusty winds whip around the farmhouses. His hunger is a pain, like the pain of his steady gaze, of his constantly straining ears. It gnaws at his insides and makes a fever rise. Hunger amplifies everything. Each sound, each cracking noise outside reverberates within him and makes him shudder despite the infant's nearly unbroken cries. Now there is hate and fear. Nick had never felt that before, not to this extent. It was deep in his body, way down inside of him, and now it was welling up, making growling sounds in his throat, bristling all the hair on his back, shrinking the black dot of the pupils in his yellow eyes even further. Every muscle in his body was coiled, ready to spring.

It was the baby's crying that awoke the hate and the fear. The cries mingle with the painful anticipation, with his painful jaws, with the parched feeling of his tongue and lips. The cries mingle with the immense emptiness that is digging a deep pit at the very core of his body.

Outside the sun burns down on the aluminum hull of the mobile home. Burns down on the charred trees imprisoned in the earth, burns down on the dusty stones of the river. Elsewhere, the automobiles roll along in the light, windows blinded, rushing toward an inexistent destiny.

Maybe, in the large cement and corrugated iron supermarket near the highway, Liana is roaming through the aisles filled with merchandise: multicolored cans, packages, meat wrapped in cellophane, fruit that is too red or too yellow, or towering cliffs of bottles filled with magical and forbidden liquids. She walks straight ahead, and the light from the neon tubes illuminates her weary face, her sunken eyes, her straw-colored hair. She wanders around aimlessly in the aisles, bumping into people and things without recognizing them. She walks from one end to the other of the large store without touching anything, without looking at anything because nothing can ever be hers anymore, because she no longer has anything.

The next second she thinks of the social worker's face, of her gold-rimmed glasses; she even hears the sound of her voice in her ears, but as hard as she tries to listen, she can't understand what the soft voice is saying. So she steps up her pace, trying to flee her anxiety, trying to hide. But there is light everywhere in the large empty store; she can't get away from it. It tightens around her throat and temples, it makes her legs tremble beneath her. Now she knows that there is no one but the social worker, no other name in the world, there, right next to Liana, and she won't be able to find her.

The young woman walks through the aisles of the supermarket for a long time, in the cold light of the neon lamps. The people don't look at her; they're too busy looking at the cakes, the fruits, the bars of soap, the clothing; their faces are meat-colored, their eyes are as shiny as bottle caps, their hands snatch out and carry away greedily.

Then all of a sudden she realizes that she is not looking for anything but the exit, a door, anywhere to flee, go outside. She has to get out, as quickly as possible; she knows how terribly urgent it is, the danger threatening back there in the mobile home.

She stops before a young, dark-haired woman with very white skin standing by the magazine rack. She'd like to ask the woman to help her, right away, because her eyes can't find the exit. She'd like to tell the woman about her child, left alone in the metal hull back there, the child that they're going to come and get, that they're going to take away, that they're going to devour. But the words won't come out of her throat. They are locked up in her body; they're so painful that her lips are quivering and tears fill her eyes, run down her cheeks.

The pale young woman looks at her for a moment without saying anything; then she hurries quickly away. Through her tears, Liana sees her turning in and out of the aisles as if she were trying to give her the slip.

Outside the sunlight is even brighter. It scorches and bleaches everything out – the stones, the earth, the leaves of the trees. There's cement dust lying on the roofs of the houses, something like a fine veil clouding the cruel blue sky. On the highway's slow-moving loops, the shells of the cars are gleaming. The wind carries over brief snatches of motors growling, of trucks roaring or horns honking like bellowing animals. Then they fade away. Everything is like that, coming in waves, unsure, flickering on and off. There is so much loneliness, so much hunger. . . . There is so much light at the deserted mouth of the river and in the vacant lot; standing alone, like the abandoned fuselage of an airplane, the aluminum hull of the mobile home is balanced precariously on its brick stays. Despite everything, despite violence and murder, there is no noise out here, except every now and again the rumbling of the highway and the barking of the farm dogs.

Daylight is waning when Liana arrives. She walks slowly across the vacant lot. She's not carrying any packages. Her clothing is covered with white dust, and she's limping a little because she's broken the heel of one shoe. Her face is twisted with worry, but she knows what she has to do now; she's finally understood. Maybe it's already too late; maybe they've set out already, with Simon or the young woman with gold-rimmed glasses leading the way. Or maybe the guardian of the vacant lot will show up with his double-barreled shotgun and his hunter's cap pushed down over his ears. They'll surely be coming now, before nightfall, to kill the dog and carry the baby off to their hospital and lock her away in a large white room with glossy walls that no one can ever escape.

Limping, she hurries toward the mobile home, steps up on the stair, opens the door. In one leap the large wolf dog is standing at her side, hair bristling, eyes glimmering, because he understands.

Together, the young woman and the dog walk across the vacant lot. Liana is hugging the baby tightly; it is wrapped in the bath towel. The baby is nursing as she walks, and in spite of her weariness, the feeling of the milk flowing out makes Liana feel calmer.

They walk along like that for a long time, until it is pitch dark. Now, they are on the banks of the river, on the dusty gravel beaches. There is the sound of a trickle of water running somewhere. Off in the distance, motors rumble on the highway viaduct. Here, the night air is cool and breezy; mosquitoes dance invisibly. Liana pulls the bath towel down over the baby's sleeping face. Without making a sound, Nick has slipped away into the scrub along the banks of the river; he's off to hunt rabbits and chickens on the farms. He'll be back at dawn, exhausted and stuffed, and his eyes will shine out in the shadows like two stars, as if their light were enough to keep the men who are searching for them at bay for a few more hours.

The Escapee

JUST BEFORE DAWN, Tayar comes out above the tree line. He has been walking all night, making only one stop at a roadside café just long enough to swallow a cup of bitter coffee that burned his throat. The road that snakes its way along the floor of the valley brought him up as far as the hills buttressing the high mountains. Tayar forded the stream just below the bridge and climbed up the old terraced groves of olive trees until he came to the narrow road that twisted its way up toward the mountaintop. Now he's standing facing the high limestone plateau, and the black of night is turning a slow gray.

The air is cold – a dry, biting kind of cold. All he is wearing are the regulation shirt-jacket and gray cloth trousers. His bare feet are pushed into a pair of laceless high-top sneakers. Weariness from the long walk weighs on him, makes him stumble. He's shivering with cold. Leaving the road, he walks out into the bushes, over the rocks that crumble and roll underfoot. He squats down to urinate in a shallow depression in the land. He looks about at the surroundings. To the east, whence he came, a slow splash is spreading across the sky, a pallid yellow glow in which the horizon is visible, the jagged rocks, the branches of dwarf trees.

Up here, the silence is vast. Tayar notices it for the first time. It's an emptiness pushing in on his eardrums, tightening around his head. Here, there are no bird songs or insect calls, nothing to greet the coming day. Only the faint wailing of the wind blowing over the high limestone plateau – the wind, coming and going like an icy breath. Tayar thinks of the sea, back there, all the way down at the bottom; he thinks of the sleepy gardens, of the buildings. They're so far away now, so small, hardly even anthills, wasps' nests; it is difficult to recall what they're like.

Tayar walks on, drunk with sleep. His eyes scan the ground for a bit of shelter, a little place in which to sleep. He knows that he will at last be able to sleep up here. No one will come looking for him. He's very familiar with this country, without ever having been here before. It's just like the land across the sea, exactly the same: boulders, thorn bushes, crevasses, rockslides. Totally deserted. Back when he was with his brother and they tended the flocks together, he used to walk here, in this very place. He remembers it perfectly well. And that's why, even though the night still half shrouds everything, he finds the shelter he's looking for: a rocky, wind-worn outcrop and the scraggly branches of a twisted shrub. Tayar hacks at the sharp stones and rolls them away with his heels, digs out a shallow spot in the stony soil. Then he squats down, leaning his back up against the rock wall, and wraps his arms around himself to keep in the body heat. That was how he used to sleep in the old days, with his brother and his Uncle Raïs, when they had to sleep out of doors in winter.

Tayar is breathing slowly to check the nervous trembling of his body, to stop his jaws from chattering. Pillowing his left cheek against his shoulder, eyes closed, he falls asleep just as the red light of the new day rises before him, magnificently illuminating the high, lonely plateau.

He sleeps in that way for a long time, without moving, breathing slowly. The bright sunlight falls upon his face and body, but it doesn't awaken him. Asleep, he is just like the gray stones that are strewn all around. His bony face is the color of earth; his black hair stirs on his forehead with the wind. His body is long and thin in the overly large clothing.

As he sleeps, Tayar is completely motionless, just like the time long ago in the Chélia Mountains when he and his brother lay hidden amid the blocks of rock. The goats and sheep had tripped off down the rocky slope to the wadi, and the sun was high up in the cloudless sky, just as it is today. Some birds flew past very quickly, in little twittering groups; his brother rose silently to his feet, trying to see where they would land. They were desert quail, as fleeting and elusive as flies.

Then Tayar awoke in turn, without really knowing why; perhaps it was simply because his brother was staring at him in silence, and that look was like a finger pushing against his chest. Very softly, like a murmur, he said, "Aazi," and together they ran barefoot, scampering down the slopes of the mountain all the way to the wadi, where the sheep had already found their shady spot for the sunny day.

The water of the torrent sparkled in the light. It leapt white and frothy over the smooth stones, flowed down toward the valley amidst tufts of euphorbia and scrawny acacias. Then the sky turned a deeper, almost dark, blue. The two boys shed their worn woolen tunics and bathed, stretching themselves out as the clear water of the torrent ran over their shoulders, into their ears and mouths. Lying flat on their stomachs, they let themselves go sliding gently down over the smooth shingles, laughing. When they stood in the sun to dry, his brother covered his newly circumcised penis with his hand. They talked a little – about what? The sheep and the goats wandered back upstream in search of fresh young plants. The flies and the gnats were already out, as if they had sprung from the euphorbia leaves; they went buzzing around the children's hair, biting them on the backs of their arms. Or sometimes there was the stinging bite of a horsefly as it landed lightly on their shoulders. So then they hurried to get dressed again, pull on the woolen tunics that clung to their wet skin. When the sun had climbed halfway to its peak, the older boy took the provisions out of the leather pouch: the heavy, plain bread, the dried dates and figs, the salty cheese, the goatskin filled with rancid butter. They ate hastily, each facing in a different direction, not saying a word. The sun burned down hotly, shrinking the shadows. The boys' faces were almost black; their eyes disappeared into dark sockets. When evening returned and the sun was nearing the hilltops, the boys climbed back up the slope of the mountain, chasing the animals before them, throwing stones. Up at the top, on the plateau, they sought out a new niche for the night, in the shelter of a shriveled tree or up against the cracked wall of an old, wind-worn boulder, and they curled up there after having cleared away the flints and rooted out the scorpions. Then they wrapped their arms around themselves, pillowing their heads on their shoulders, as the earth grew steadily colder.

Tayar awakens before noon. Opening his eyes, he is instantly stricken by the immense whiteness, the sun glinting off limestone. The sky is a very pale blue, almost white. The light is a stabbing pain behind his eyes; it's shattering. Tayar can feel tears rolling down his cheeks. With great difficulty, he succeeds in untangling the knot of his arms around his body, stretches his legs. The wind is still blowing in the same direction, whistling through the branches of the shriveled tree.

Tayar rises to his feet, staggers. He takes a few steps, squats to urinate. He's had nothing to drink since the day before, and his urine is dark and smelly. He searches the horizon, trying to sense if there is water anywhere. Like in the old days, his nostrils flare to pick up the smell of water. There are no shadows, not even an outcrop of plants or a crevasse. The limestone plateau is desolate and dry, swept with wind and light.

Tayar begins walking again. He walks straight ahead. The light is as harsh as stone, as harsh as the sky. But after having been locked up in prison for all those days, in that dark cell; after the damp, stinking passageways, where the air flickers with the glow of neon tubes; after all the stamping footsteps, the voices, the slamming doors, always banging three times, like this: bam! bam-bam! Tayar loves this harshness, this stony, windy silence, this vast, cloudless sky, where only one sun burns.

Hunger, thirst and fatigue have cleansed him of all that. He can feel the prison memories leaving him. Perhaps he should have come up here right away. Down in the gray haze of town, fear, hate, resentment are everywhere. Tayar thinks of Mariem, hiding in a hotel room because she thinks he's going to come and take revenge, kill her with his switchblade. She knows now that he escaped; she must have heard about it. The police probably got her that room, in a dingy hotel near the train station because they too think he'll try and get even; they've laid their trap. Yes, that's it; the rat trap is set; they're waiting for him, holed up in a van somewhere on the street. Or else at the bar across the street from the station, they're drinking coffee and beer all day long waiting for him. Tayar almost laughs when he thinks of the police hiding there, waiting to ambush him.

The air is cold up here, in spite of the blinding sun. Very slowly, in order to save strength, Tayar makes his way up toward the top of the limestone plateau, toward what seems to be a sheer cliff face forming a sort of giant step. Thorn bushes scratch his legs, tear the cloth of the gray trousers. Even though there's not a soul up there, Tayar is careful not to leave any traces, not to break the branches of the bushes, not to displace the small stones in the dry dirt. Instinctively, he's picked up his old habits again, those he had forgotten about while living in the city, bending slightly forward to be less visible, to offer the least resistance to the wind, arms held close to his sides, breathing through his nose to keep his throat from getting dry, always poised to leap into a hole in the ground for cover.

The nearer he draws to the rocky cliff, the more strongly his instincts tell him there is water somewhere at the top. He can't see it or hear it, but he can feel it in his bones, like a distant memory. He scales the cliff with great difficulty; some rocks tumble down, making a noise that clatters across the vast stone landscape. Tayar freezes, crouching against the rocks, waiting for silence to return.

Up this high, even the light is more pervasive. Nothing separates him from the sky now. The expanse of the limestone plateau is immense; the sky, a pale blue at the horizon, deep as night at its zenith. The wind stirs through the brush, rustles the dry, withered leaves of the shrubs. The dirt between the stones is gray, white, the color of saltpeter. Up here, in spite of the sun, Tayar can feel the chill of open space, the wind. It is a bitter and desiccating wind, blowing very hard, coming from the depths of the atmosphere. Tayar stretches out on the ground to rest, staring up at the sky. He doesn't know what he should do anymore, where he should go. He doesn't even know why he came up here anymore when he fled the big city and all its familiar streets. He thinks briefly of Mariem; he pictures her face, her body, her legs walking along, her shiny yellow hair. But the image quickly vanishes, is wiped away with the sky and the wind.

Tayar can feel every tortured muscle in his body. There's also that pain deep in his lungs – a sharp, burning pain throbbing out in feverish waves. He turns over on his stomach; he looks at the ground and the bushes all around him. There are flat little gnats flying about the tufts of euphorbia. There's also a bee being swept away on the wind. And a large black ant running along the dusty ground. Tayar watches it intently, as though it were the last living thing around. The ant runs toward his face, then, noticing him, hesitates and takes off in the opposite direction. Tayar feels happy watching it. He rolls over on his side to better see it running away.

Suddenly, he is seeing something else. He is with his Uncle Raïs on Chélia Mountain, on the side of the setting sun. It was so long ago that Tayar doesn't even know what the two of them were doing there anymore, lying so still in the stones, holding their breaths, watching. They had walked a long way through the brush, for Uncle Raïs's clothes are torn and dust-covered, and Tayar's feet are all bloody. They had walked for days; they're fleeing some danger that Tayar doesn't understand. Tayar knows that he mustn't talk. The sun is burning his neck and back, but the wind is cold; it stirs through the blades of grass and the leaves of the bushes. Keep quiet, be as mute as the mountain rocks, silent as a hare. Both of them, Uncle Raïs and the boy, are staring intently at several strange black spots moving along at the foot of the mountain, following the dry streambed: men.

They are soldiers from the outpost at Lambessa, on patrol in search of fugitives. They're so far away that their faces can't be seen. Only the dark green splotches of their uniforms and their machine guns. The men move slowly forward along the floor of the valley, without stopping, without looking up. Is it because they're afraid also? Tayar would like to ask his uncle, but he dares not speak, not even in a whisper.

Fear is everywhere up here on the mountain. It's in every white stone, every tuft of euphorbia, every thorn bush; it's in the bed of the wadi, where the dark soldiers are moving slowly along like ants. It's in the distant hills, shaded in purple; it's in the infinite sky, like a hovering bird of prey. It makes a terrifying silence, a silence that nothing can break, a silence that creeps into your body and chills you to the bone.

Lying there on the limestone plateau, Tayar is conscious of that silence. Perhaps the soldiers are coming, right now, following his trail through the patches of sand, keeping an eye out for broken branches, displaced stones, small screes.

At the head of the column of soldiers there is a big dog. Tayar has never seen such a large one before. He can see it clearly, pulling on the leash wrapped about the soldier's hand. The dog too is searching, sniffing the stones of the ravine. At times it stops, its nose in the air, as if it has smelled something, and Tayar thinks that it's going to look over in their direction, bark. But the big dog starts out again, running off in a bit of a zigzag, dragging the men along at a run in its wake, and in spite of the fear, Tayar wants to laugh. It's because the fear doesn't stem from the men; it exists by itself; it is born of the mountain wilderness, the white stones, the bushes whose leaves tremble with the wind, the barren sky with the ever-present sun.

Tayar shudders, shakes his head violently to rid himself of the vision of the mountain. He gets heavily back to his feet and begins walking again over the limestone plateau. His breath is wheezing in his lungs; there is kind of a red veil undulating right beneath his eyes, close to the ground, like a blood-filled lake.

It's because he's had nothing to eat or drink for a long time. Tayar knows that if he doesn't find a little water soon, he won't be able to walk any farther. His feverish eyes scour the white landscape intently. The noon sun is lighting up every stone, every tree, leaving no shadows.

Then directly in front of him, down on a slightly lower level, he spots a dark patch, the kind made by bushes with still-green leaves, with dark branches. The bushes form a circle around a depression that can barely be seen. Tayar staggers over in that direction. There is water over there, for sure, somewhere. Instincts born long before his life began tell him he will find water there, that it is waiting for him.

It is a dark mouth, opening in the rocky surface. Despite the aridity of the surroundings, the air seems moist here, like the air on the floor of a valley. There are shrubs all around the mouth, like a bristling, woolly fleece, slanting with the wind. As he draws nearer, Tayar can see that the opening is very large, like a crater. On the slope there are the ruins of a stone hut and a drinking hole filled with water. Tayar climbs down into the natural depression; he cannot take his eyes from it: the large black pool, with the light from the sky bouncing off its surface, still as a mirror. He leans over the water, trembling with fatigue, and, without even using his hands, drinks deeply.

Inside the basin there is not a sound. Only the wind whistling through the branches of the thorn bushes. Up above, the sky is bright, blinding. Tayar lies down on the mossy grass by the hut. The sun burns on his face and hands. To ease his exhaustion and his loneliness, Tayar hums a little tune at the back of his throat, just as he used to in the old days, curled up against a rock on the slopes of Chélia.

Is he dreaming? He's all alone in the vastness of these mountains. The sun is beating ruthlessly down. There is not a cloud in the sky, not a sound to be heard.

The child is waiting there, still clinging to hope, lying on the ground. No one is going to come anymore, not now, not a soul. Uncle Raïs went off yesterday, or maybe it was the day before. He left his pouch and goatskin here so that he could walk faster. He said he was going as far as Lambessa, after stopping over at the ruins of Timgad, to pick up some money and supplies and get the messages that had been left for him. He said to wait for him, without moving. Don't move, Aazi, so that the soldiers' dogs won't hear you. Don't move; don't get up. Don't talk, and above all don't call out, Aazi, but wait there, lying on the ground, hidden amid the rocks and the bushes. What should he do? The child is trembling in spite of the sun. The barren sky weighs so heavily upon him; the light blinds him, parches his throat. From time to time, like the sun glinting out from behind a hawk's wing, he catches sight of something resembling the sign of fear. The sign of death is there. It's a sign you see when you close your eyes, a terrifying mark. The silence is endless. The child cannot stand up, cannot call out; he must not. The soldiers are like insects: first there's no sign of them, then all of a sudden they're there, and you can't understand where they came from. The soldiers are walking along the cracks in the earth, just like ants. Where do they come from? What do they want? What are they looking for? Lying upon the blistering earth, Tayar covers his head with his arms. Fever is throbbing in his temples, or is it the hot noon sun? The day has been ablaze for such a long time now, without ever burning out, as though night should never come again. Thirst is immense; it's like a shudder running all along his skin. Slowly the boy turns around, stretches his hand out toward the empty goatskin. It's dry, shriveled like a dead teat. Down there in the scorched ravine runs the sparkling water of the wadi. Tayar can hear it distinctly; its song is as clear as a bird's, beautiful and pure. Hearing the sound of it refreshes him, brings some strength back to his body. But he mustn't move, mustn't get up. It's not the sound of water that you're hearing, Aazi. It's a trap laid by a soldier. He's made a lure out of a bit of elder branch, and he's singing the water song to coax people he wants to kill into coming closer. If Tayar goes down from the mountain, if he goes near the wadi to drink, the big dog will leap upon him, snarling, and all the soldiers will be standing by while the dog devours him.

The sun has gone down toward the horizon now, and Tayar starts walking again. After having slept on the floor of the basin, he feels much better. Before leaving the basin, he took a few more swallows from the waterhole. The cold water seemed heavy to him, bitter, metallic tasting, but it brought him new strength.

Tayar walks into the sun, blinded, stumbling over the stones. He follows an old trail that runs across the limestone plateau and comes to an end looking out over a large ravine, already deep in shadow. On the far side of the ravine is the slope leading down to Calern; on his right, the chaotic peaks of Cheiron; on his left, down in the dale, barely visible in the smoke-colored shadows, the farms of Saint-Lambert.

Still that silence, like a threat. The cold wind blows ever harder, as though borne on the gathering night. Maybe there are even dogs barking down on the farms in the valley, and Tayar thinks that they are barking at him, just as they did in the old days. But the silence clamps back down again as always, drowning out any sounds of life. All that is left are the sounds of things, very faint, the cracking of rocks, bushes rustling in the wind.

The light is fading as Tayar turns back from the edge of the ravine. It's been a long time since he's eaten, and he no longer has the strength to scale the rockslides. He's forced to sit down, clinging to the rocks, with his heart pounding heavily. Each time he stops, he squats down on his haunches, just as he used to do in the high lands up on Chélia. He strains to listen as best he can, being alert to the slightest sound.

It is the sound of his uncle's footsteps that he is listening for, perhaps, or the sound of his voice, somewhat gruff and muffled, calling out as he arrives, "Aazi! . . . Aazi!" But it's not his uncle. It's his sister Horriya and he has always loved her name because of what it means: freedom.

She's coming over to him; he can see her in the dim evening light. She's walking up to him, wrapped in her black veil. When she is only a few steps away, she pulls away the veil, uncovering her handsome face, as smooth as copper.

She's not keeping under cover. She's not afraid of anyone. She stops in front of Tayar and pulls her veil up again; in the crook of her right arm is a loaf of black bread and a goatskin of buttermilk. Kneeling down beside him, she touches his brow with her cool hand, and instantly the burning heat of the sun subsides, as if a cloud were passing overhead. She helps the child to sit up, cradling the back of his head as he drinks the buttermilk. Then he vomits because it has been too long since he's had either food or drink. Horriya wipes his mouth with her veil, saying nothing, and he drinks again. The smooth, sour milk is so invigorating that it makes him tremble.

She feeds him little pieces of bread, as if to a baby. She says a few words in her soothing voice, but her face is sad. Tayar understands in a flash that his Uncle Raïs is dead. The soldiers killed him over near the ruins of Timgad. But he's so tired that it's all the same to him, and he doesn't ask any questions.

But the sky is even emptier, vaster, whiter. The sun has slid down onto the line of mountains at the horizon. Tayar knows that night will fall very suddenly once it goes behind the peaks of Thiey and l'Audibergue. Hurriedly, he tries to get back to the shelter of the basin.

But he has lost the way. He wanders aimlessly around under the yellow sky, over the expanse of black and white stones.

Bushes are very infrequent. There are long, dry-stone walls stretching all the way to the other end of the plateau for no apparent reason. Struggling along, Tayar follows them. Thirst and hunger are stabbing pains. They shoot out from the sharp stones, from the sky, from the bushes. Squatting down on his haunches for a moment to rest, Tayar's hands brush against the already cold stones.

Now he remembers; it was his Uncle Raïs who had first told him about it, but he had already known it, as though it were something he had known from birth. Hurriedly, he searches among the stones until he finds a large one in a triangle shape. This is the one, the one he'd heard people in the old days call "the hunger stone." His Uncle Raïs used to tell him about it, he remembers; he would point out the stone to him and laugh, and Tayar would know that it was no ordinary stone. This was a stone that held a secret, a spirit, when one encountered it along the path.

Tayar unbuttons his regulation shirt-jacket and presses the point of the stone against his skin, right where the knot of pain is throbbing, very near his heart. The coldness of the stone makes him swoon, but he holds it very tightly in his arms, pressing in. The pointed part of the stone bites into his flesh. He holds the stone so tightly against his body that he moans with pain. But his arms pay no attention to the pain.

The stone is pushing so hard against his diaphragm that Tayar can hardly breathe. He gets to his feet, doubled over, weighted down, and begins walking again over the limestone plateau. Now the stone is helping him, filling him with its cold strength, wiping away the hunger and the pain.

Just as night begins to fall, Tayar catches sight of the basin. Inside he can see the hut, like a stone igloo. Farther out is the rocky spine of the mountains and perhaps, already immersed in night, studded with far-away stars glittering from the depths of the shadows, the valley of the Loup River.

The soft dusk light is still hovering at the edge of the basin. Tayar moves down toward the hut; he stares at the low door opening into darkness. He hesitates because it looks so much like the tomb of a magician. As he stoops to enter the stone hut, his hands are trembling. The mud floor is clean except for the remnants of an old fire, of which only a few ashes are left.

Tayar sits down in the doorway to the hut, leaning over the hunger stone. Feebly, he gathers some bits of wood, twigs, leaves, to make a fire. Then he remembers that he no longer has any matches. They took them away from him when he went to prison. In any case, the wood in the hut might have been too damp, and he might not even know how to build a fire anymore. In the old days, in their hideouts up on Chélia Mountain, his brother would bring back big branches, lichens resembling long strands of hair, and he'd squat down on his haunches to light the fire.

It's down at the bottom of a valley, not far from the ruins of Timgad. The sheep are standing in a circle around a dry tree, as though it were their true master and not the children in rags who had chased after them, throwing stones all day. They are surrounded by the pitch black, star-filled night. The shrill calls of insects are everywhere. The cold wind is blowing, just as it is here, and it's because of the wind that the sheep are all huddling up against the bark of the old, lightning-struck tree.

When the flame jumps from between the boy's nimble fingers, vibrant, joyous, just like a wild animal, Tayar stares at it, totally absorbed. He is happy, filled with such an intense elation that he cannot move a muscle or say a word. He can only stare, totally spellbound, drunk with the sight of the flames. His brother laughs, whoops, throwing into the flames large branches of evergreen oak that explode, sending clouds of sparks into the sky. "Come, Aazi!" he says. "Come and help me!" So then he too feeds the fire, with twigs, dried grasses, roots still covered with red earth, anything he can find. The fire is voracious; it devours everything very quickly; it throws out billows of smoke into the flickering light. Insects come to die in the fire; long, winged ants, streaking across the night, sizzle in the flames. Tayar watches his brother's face. It is a reddish brown; it too is the color of fire, and his curls have copper highlights. But most of all, his eyes are like fire, as if embers glowed out from behind them in the night. He runs and dances about the fire. He speaks to it as though it really were an animal, shouting out strange, guttural-sounding commands from time to time: "Naoh! Narr! – " Or cursing it because he's burned himself getting too near the flame to throw on a branch.

And when the fire is blazing high and it has devoured the whole supply of branches, the two children sit down facing it, opposite the smoke, and watch it slowly die while the cold night creeps gradually back in, up their backs, through their hair, into the earth between their fingers.

Tayar is dreaming of fire, his eyes staring blankly into the night. Sitting down in the basin, sheltered from the wind, he can see only the rim of the crater standing out against the pale sky. Tayar feels cut off from human beings. He hasn't felt this lonely for such a long time that it makes him dizzy. Slowly, still hugging the hunger stone, Tayar leaves the hut and makes his way down to the bottom of the basin. He crawls along on all fours like a dog, with his head thrown back to see the star filled sky. The floor of the basin is covered with a soft carpet of grass that holds in the day's heat like a woolen fleece.

The wind is blowing over the top of the crater, great gusts that come from the depths of space. There is nothing but the sound of the lashing wind and the cold. Tayar remains curled up for a long time, not moving, watching the stars. Gradually, he recalls the positions of the stars in the sky in the old days; he recognizes them one by one, without knowing their names or anything about them. Then comes the soft glow of the rising moon, over in the east, a broad white patch spreading across the sky. It was all so long ago; Tayar had forgotten what it was like. But it's more powerful than everything in his life put together; it comes back in full force, draining and purifying him just as the hunger and the thirst had done.

Tayar remains very still in order to keep the hunger stone in place. The waterhole for sheep is up near the ruined hut. Tayar walks slowly over to the pool; he drinks again of the dark, muddy water. Then he goes to the back of the hut to sleep. His eyes don't close. They remain fixed on the black rim of the crater, cutting out a circle of sky. Tayar listens to the wind as if he were on a ship bound for the unknown.

When the sun reappears in the cloudless sky, Tayar goes to sit on the edge of the crater. He stares at the rocky plain stretching out toward the rugged mountains. There are dry-stone walls everywhere. Here and there, out in the distance, dark splotches mark the craters of other basins.

The silence is so complete, so heavy, that Tayar doesn't hear the young boy approach. He is a strong child of twelve or thirteen, with very brown skin and black, wind-mussed hair. Now he's standing on the other side of the crater, with his back to the sun. He's wearing a ski jacket that is a bit too large. Keeping very still, he stands there, looking at Tayar with his hands in his pockets.

Tayar sees him. He tries to get up, but the weight of the stone pressing against his stomach makes him fall back down. For a few seconds, Tayar thinks he would like to kill the boy who is staring at him. But that's impossible now. He puts his hand into the pocket of his trousers and feels with the tips of his fingers the little switchblade that Frank gave him before he went on the run. It's a small knife with a plastic handle and a thin, sharp blade, and when he first took it in his hand,

Tayar thought of Mariem. Now he knows perfectly well that he can't use it anymore. He hasn't the strength left. The wind, the chill of night, the silence, and the hunger have all robbed him of any desire for revenge.

Tayar looks at the young boy, who resembles him, standing on the far side of the basin. He says, "Come, come!" with his hand. The boy watches for some time, not moving, then walks around the crater, unhurriedly, with his hands in his pockets. His face is very dark; there is a metallic glint in his black eyes.

Tayar watches anxiously as he draws nearer. It's been such a long time since he has seen a human face. The boy stops a few paces away from him. He studies Tayar closely. He's pretending not to be afraid, with his hands in his pockets, but he is poised to leap backward at the slightest sign of danger.

"What's your name?" says Tayar. It's difficult for him to speak because of the hunger stone pushed against his diaphragm. And also because it's been a long time since he has spoken and the words are all dried up in his throat.

The boy doesn't answer. He just says, "Are you hurt?"

"I spent the night here," says Tayar. "You don't have anything to eat do you? I'm hungry."

The boy looks at the stone that Tayar is holding against his stomach. "What's that for?"

"It's nothing," replies Tayar. He lets the stone fall to the ground beside him. "It's just a gimmick for not feeling hungry."

The boy doesn't say anything more. He just stands there staring, leaning his body slightly to one side, and suddenly Tayar is terrified of the silence; he wants the child to stay with him. He struggles to pull the little knife with the plastic handle out of his pocket and holds it out to the boy:

"Listen, I don't have any money left, but I'll give you the knife. Bring me some food, I'm very hungry. I haven't eaten for several days."

The young boy doesn't move, doesn't answer. His dark shape is silhouetted against the sunny sky, and Tayar can't see his face. All of a sudden the boy leaves, walks away from the basin without looking back. Tayar cries out to him, and his voice croaks:

"Where are you going? Hey! come back!"

Silence spreads back over the limestone plateau. Tayar's head begins to reel again, and he goes back down to the bottom of the basin. Maybe it's because the pain is returning to his body now that he's lost the hunger stone.

All day, Tayar watches the spot on the rim of the crater where the young boy had appeared. At times, he believes he sees the motionless figure standing against the sky, with his dark face and his hair the color of meadow grass shining in the sun. He's a thin child, with a sober face and dark eyes hidden deep in their dark sockets. His thin lips are tightened into a mute expression. Tayar watches him from the floor of the basin with feverish eyes. He knows him well; he recognizes him. The child resembles him. He is like an exact reflection of himself. He is wearing the same clothes – the long woolen tunic, frayed about the neck, floating around his thin body, describing the shape of his legs. He's standing barefooted on the sharp stones, and his hair is blowing in the wind, as dark and shiny as meadow grass.

When he recognizes the boy, Tayar feels overcome with a strange sort of giddiness that dispels all pain. The gnawing hunger stops, and his breath comes more easily, filling his chest with a prolonged sigh. Without knowing how, he finds himself standing on the high limestone plateau, feeling the strong wind in his face. He can see the slope opposite him, where the goat path runs zigzagging through the brush and the rockslides down to the bed of the wadi.

It is a huge cleft in the mountain, filled with a vibrant light that seems as though it should never end. Tayar is leaning forward, his whole being intent upon gazing into the emptiness. The pink sandstone and quartz of the mountain are glittering as if for the dawning of a new day. The sky is blue. There isn't a sound, only the breath of the wind in his ears, the hissing sound of sand crumbling. Nothing is stirring. Not a bird or any earthbound creature. The light opens out its path to the horizon, and Tayar is gliding along that path. He leaves himself and spreads out to all points of the valley, all the way out to the horizon. He can see the red stones of the ruins of Timgad, like broken termite mounds, and the palms of the oasis, where a fine, steamy mist floats, lighter than a cloud of smoke.

Still farther out, the path of light guides him to the mud house on the edge of the wadi. But the house is abandoned. The gate of branches that closed the pen is flung to the ground; all the sheep and goats are gone. Tayar looks at all of that dust with pained alertness, and every stone, every inch of the mud walls, every dead branch re-opens old wounds in him. The stony landscape around the house opens out infinitely; the cold desert wind blows across the face of the motionless man.

Slowly, hour by hour, the sun moves back down toward the horizon. The night sets in, pitch black at first, flooding the limestone plateau with its bitter cold. Tayar has crawled all the way to the rim of the basin, not far from the hut, but the icy wind pushes him back, and he slips slowly down again to the floor of the crater; he curls himself up in the damp grass. He is still thinking about the path of light that he saw just a moment ago, the path that made the young boy who so resembles him appear. But now everything has vanished with the cold.

The stars come out very faintly, then grow brighter and brighter. Never had they shone so brightly before. Resting his head on the grass, Tayar watches them in delight. Just as he had the night before, he recognizes them. He finds their positions in the sky, the patterns they make, right down to the very smallest ones that barely glimmer, so low and close to the earth. Tonight, there is something different about them, as though they carried a hidden message. A sort of music that goes straight to the very core of his being and makes him restless. Tayar watches the path of stars flowing across the black sky; he listens to their shrill, buoyant song scattering into the void. The sky is all encompassing; it covers everything, and below it, time is eradicated in a multiple vortex. Endlessly, new patterns, new stars appear. Tayar is aware that he no longer has a face or a body but that he's become a steady pinpoint in the night, there, upon the cold earth. Without closing his eyes, he slips, leaden, into an ice-cold sleep that slows his heartbeat and respiration. Above him, the stars are quick and intense with life, dazzlingly bright, their strident songs interweaving in the night, like the calls of insects.

At daybreak, moisture from the night trickles down Tayar's face. The first rays of light stir him from his dream and – indistinctly at first, then more and more clearly – he sees the silhouette of the boy who resembles him. The young boy is standing poised on the rim of the crater, and the sunlight makes his face seem even darker, almost black. His hair is the color of burnt grass.

The child is standing still, staring at him. Tayar would like to tell him to come over, motion to him just as he had yesterday, but he can't move anymore. The cold night has made him as heavy as stone. He can only stare with his eyes to call for help.

In a few leaps, the boy has reached him at the bottom of the basin. He pulls out a piece of bread, an orange, and a knife from his jacket pocket. He puts them down next to Tayar without saying anything.

When he sees that Tayar can't move, he breaks off a bit of bread and puts it into the man's mouth. Then he peels the orange and gives him a section. The juice runs into Tayar's throat, and strength gradually returns to his body. Trembling, he tries to prop himself on his elbows. The first rays of the sun are lighting the rim of the crater and the dark bushes, shivering in the wind. Tayar eats some more bread; he sucks the sections of orange and spits out the skin.

"Are you hungry?"

Tayar nods his head, still eating.

"Are you cold?"

The boy takes off his jacket and drapes it over the man's chest, wrapping the sleeves around either side of his neck.

"Are you hurt?" the boy asks again. There's no more fear in his voice, only concern. Tayar answers no with a shake of his head. The juice from the orange is filling his mouth, bringing life back to his face, to his insides.

"What's your name?"

Tayar tries to speak, but his voice is so weak that he alone can hear it. The boy is leaning over him; his eyes shine out in his dark face with a glow that seems to come from within. He isn't saying anything; he's just looking at Tayar, and the light from the boy's eyes gives him new strength, just as nourishment would.

Tayar closes his eyes, just for an instant. He's forgetting everything now – the prison cell with grimy walls, the smell of mildew and urine, the sound of footsteps echoing in the long corridors, over his head, under his bed, everywhere, the steely stamping of heels walking the corridors interminably. It is all finally fading away, along with the buzzing sound of the neon tubes, the creaking gates, and that dreaded sound of doors slamming, always banging three times, like this: bam! bam-bam! The sound of a heart beating, of doors slamming, of pistol shots. Here, all of that is fading away in the soft morning light up on the limestone plateau, in the gaze of the child who is kneeling beside him. He opens his eyes, sees the motionless silhouette of the boy, his hair gleaming in the sun like meadow grass. Weakly, he says, "Aazi – "

and gives a silent little laugh. His hand lifts to catch hold of the boy's fingers; suddenly the child leaps to his feet, stands there, poised for an instant, muscles coiled, ready to flee.

Pulling himself up in an effort that brings beads of sweat to his face and sets the inside of his chest on fire, Tayar watches the child running along the rim of the crater, light-footed as a young goat. The silhouette remains balanced for an instant on the sharp edge of the crater, as if the child were hesitating. Then suddenly, and Tayar can't understand how, he has vanished. Now there is nothing but the immense, barren sky, the light, the sound of the wind.

Groping about on the ground next to him, Tayar finds the pieces of bread and the moist orange skins. He tries to pick up a piece of bread, but his fingers aren't strong enough and the bread rolls away into the grass beside him. Despite the jacket over his chest, Tayar feels the cold creeping into his body, slowly taking hold of him.

Inching forward on his belly, Tayar tries to climb back up the slope of the basin. It takes him such a long time that he can no longer remember very well what happened just before. Through blurred eyes he stares straight at the sharp stones above him, the branches on the thorn bushes standing out against the white sky. At times the world seems to drain away, as though night were near, a terrifying night that would never end; other times a veil of blood covers everything, lending a lethal glow to the thorns. Slithering along on his stomach like a lizard, Tayar pulls himself slowly back up the side of the crater. The stones rip into his forearms and knees, bruising his chest and face, but he pays no heed. He can still muster one last bit of strength because he wants to see. The child has vanished, leaving behind him a trail of light. That is what Tayar wants to follow now, like a path that will lead him to the stone landscape he knows so well, to the valley opening out in the mountains, running all the way to the ends of the earth.

It's a place he never really left. Slowly, Tayar drags himself up to the rim of the crater, up to where he can see the path of light. The limestone plateau is lonely under the blue sky; the icy wind is blowing through the thorn bushes. Off in the distance, the high mountain peaks are already gray, otherworldly. Driven by the same inner force, Tayar continues crawling out onto the plateau, far from the shelter of the basin. He follows the trail of light left by the child that leads through the bushes out to the edge of the cliff. The stones wound his hands, rip his clothing, but he doesn't feel anything. He drags his body along, sometimes rising up to crawl on his hands and knees to the other end of the plateau, where all the sunlight is. He is hurrying because he knows that night will soon fall and he won't be able to resist the cold that will settle over the earth. He must reach the edge of the cliff before the sun touches the mountains or it will be too late.

As he crawls along on the ground, the smell of sheep dung mingles with that of the grass, with the fragrance of smoke wafting up from the farms nestled in the valleys.

But the sun travels quickly, plunging earthward like a dazzling vessel. The light strikes Tayar on the forehead, slowing his progress. Blinded, he closes his eyes. But he is already at the cliff's edge. Looking over, he is overcome with dizziness.

He's lying there, just as he had as a child on Mount Chélia, flat on his belly amid the stones, holding his breath. Maybe his uncle's voice is murmuring, "Don't move Aazi, don't talk. . . ."

The sun is scorching and blindingly bright, but at last Tayar sees what he is searching for: the immense valley running out to the other end of the world, the place in which every stone, every plant, every thorn bush glows in unique splendor; for in that place, light is drawn from within and not from the sky.

As he contemplates the shadowless valley, Tayar is filled with bliss. Tears fill his eyes, and for the first time in days, he no longer feels hungry. The burning sensation in the center of his chest is radiating outward like a sun.

An immense silence covers the valley. Not a bird glides overhead, not a shadow, not a fear. "Don't make a sound, Aazi, look. . . ." The sun is burning the back of his neck and his shoulders through his torn clothing. He left the goatskin over in the rocks, along with the leather pouch, so that he could walk faster. He has a long way to go before nightfall – all the way to the cave on the slopes of Chélia, where his brother and sister Horriya are waiting for him. That's all there is now; no one else exists in the world. The great open valley runs out to the other end of the world, farther than Timgad, farther than Lambessa. The child has come back to lead the way for him, to leave his beacon of light. Now Tayar need simply watch and let himself slip onto the shining way.

Tayar can't see the sun going down toward the mountains or the shadows drowning the valley. His head is resting on the ground; his hair is blowing in the wind; he is very still, as if he were asleep. And yet his eyes are open, and the sclerae gleam in the light. He is breathing very slowly, with great difficulty.

And so he doesn't see the men walking along the path between the dry-stone walls. They are wearing uniforms, and one of them is holding the leash of a great, tawny-colored dog that is sniffing about in the rocks, stopping every now and again. The men know which way to go, led by a young boy who is walking silently out in front of them. They continue across the limestone plateau toward the crater, already caught in shadow. They are hurrying silently along and, for a moment, the sound of their boots disturbs the silence of the earth.

Ariadne

ON THE BANKS of the dry riverbed stands the high-rise project. It is a city in its own right, with scores of apartment buildings – great gray concrete cliffs standing upright on the level asphalt grounds, surrounded by a sweeping landscape of rubble hills, highways, bridges, the river's dusty shingle bed, and the incinerator plant trailing its acrid, heavy cloud over the valley. Here, it's quite a distance to the sea, quite a distance to the town, quite a distance to freedom, quite a distance from simple fresh air on account of the smoke from the incinerator plant, and quite a distance from human contact, for the project looks like an abandoned town. Perhaps there really is no one there – no one in the tall gray buildings with thousands of rectangular windows, no one in the stairwells, in the elevators, and still no one in the great parking lots where the cars are parked. Perhaps all the doors and windows have been bricked up, blinded, and no one can escape from within the walls, the apartments, the basements. An yet aren't the people moving around between the great gray walls – the men, the women, the children, even the dogs occasionally – rather like shadowless ghosts, disembodied, intangible, blank-eyed beings lost in lifeless space? And they can never meet one another, never find one another. As if they had no names.

From time to time, a shadow slips by, fleeing between the white walls. Sometimes one can get a glimpse of the sky, despite the haze, despite the heavy cloud drifting down from the chimney of the incinerator plant in the west. You see airplanes too, having torn free of the clouds for an instant, drawing long, cottony filaments behind their shimmering wings.

But there are no birds around here, no flies, no grasshoppers. Now and again one finds a stray ladybug on one of the big cement parking lots. It walks along on the ground, then tries to escape, flying heavily over in the direction of the planters filled with parched earth, where a scorched geranium stands.

There are children too at times. Stopped in front of the entrances to the buildings, they've thrown their book satchels on the ground and are playing, yelling, fighting. But that doesn't last long. They enter the cubicles inside the walls, and television voices can be heard muttering, snickering, humming. Or suddenly, at nightfall, there's the shrieking sound of motorcycles, and the gang whips by at top speed, zigzagging across the parking lot, circling the lampposts. Maybe ten, twenty bikes, and all the boys wear Plexiglas masks, imitation black leather jackets, orange or multicolored helmets. The noise of their motors bounces off the concrete walls, roars through the hallways, through the underground passageways, makes a few dogs start barking. Then, all of a sudden, they're gone, and the sound of their motors fades away, snuffed out between other walls, deep in the bowels of some other basement.

Sometimes they go out beyond the incinerator plant, far into the Ariadne Valley, or else they wind their way around the curves that lead up to the cemetery; they climb Lauvette's rise. It's a strange sound, like a herd of wild beasts squalling and bellowing in the night, rolling echoes around in the dark ravines. It's a terrifying sound, for it comes from all sides at once, incomprehensible, almost supernatural.

At night, the air blows coldly between the buildings and over the parking lots, like over rocky plateaus. The sky is black, starless, moonless, with the great metal lampposts casting blinding circles of light on the asphalt. By day, the sun bounces off the concrete-colored walls, trapped by the thick layer of clouds, and the light is filled with infinite silence. There are reflections; there are shadows. Cars pass on the highway that runs along by the river and further below, on the freeway bridge. The motors rattle and roll incessantly between the high cliffs, cement trucks, trucks hauling wood, gas, bricks, trucks carrying meat or milk. Cars head out to the supermarkets or come back, windshields blind, as if no one were really driving them.

Today, Easter Monday, the huge high-rise project is even emptier, even vaster. The sky is gray; a cold wind is blowing down the dry riverbed, swelling up between the embankments, between the tall cliffs of the buildings. The white light of the clouds glints off the windows all the way up to the fifteenth floor, with flashes that seem to move, something like reflections. Faint shadows can be made out on the great empty parking lots.

The people aren't anywhere to be seen; they've disappeared. The hulls of parked cars stand alone, just like those out in the immense car graveyards a little way upriver. This is their day, a day for abandoned carcasses with no motors, no doors, no wheels, with headlights gouged out, windshields shattered, hoods gaping and showing the black holes from which their cylinder heads have been torn.

In the empty streets there are a few children running around after a black and white ball; some women have stopped by the curb and are talking. Sometimes there's music. It's coming from a window thrown wide open in spite of the cold wind – heavy music, with languid accents and an oddly high-pitched voice quavering interminably and hands clapping in rhythm. Who is that voice singing for? The silence behind it is so great, so endless! The silence comes from the treeless mountains whose crest is lost in the clouds; the silence comes from the roads, from the dry riverbed, and from the freeway on its giant pillars off in the distance. A bitter cold silence, a silence chafing with dust and cement, thick as the dark smoke billowing from the chimneys of the incinerator plant. A silence from beyond the rumbling of motors. A silence that dwells up in the hills over by the cemetery, that mingles with the acrid smell of smoke from the incinerator plant and descends heavily onto the floor of the valley, onto the project's parking lots, seeping all the way down into the depths of the dark basements.

Christine is there walking, along by the tall buildings, with her head cast down, not looking at anything, not stopping. She is tall and slim, especially in her black corduroy pants and her low-cut boots with very high heels. She's also wearing a white plastic jacket and a red and white striped sweater. Her blond hair is tied up in a ponytail, and gold-colored earrings are clipped to her ears. The cold wind comes in from the sea, out there beyond the hills, and whips along the interminable street; it blows up the river valley, raising the dust. It's still a winter wind, and Christine wraps herself tightly in her plastic jacket, holding the collar closed with her right hand as she thrusts the left one down into the back pocket of her pants, onto her buttocks.

The silence is so great that she can hear the hollow sound of her heels reverberating through the labyrinth of parking lots, bouncing off the walls of the tall buildings, and even down in the deepest of basements. But maybe it's the cold that keeps her from hearing anything else. Her heels hit the cement sidewalk with a metallic sound, hard and insistent; the sound echoes deeply through her body and in her mind.

Every now and again, as she is walking along, she tries to catch a glimpse of herself in the windows of parked vans or else in the rearview mirrors on the outside of big trucks. She tries to see herself, somewhat anxiously tilting her head a bit, squinting her eyes. Then, in the small convex mirrors, she can see her long black and white shape come dancing up as if in a blue haze. Long legs, long arms, her body splays out at the hips like a funnel, with a small pinhead of a face framed by her golden hair. Then the face grows larger, wider, until it becomes a bit deformed – a long nose, black eyes too far apart like those of a fish, a cherry-colored, smiling mouth showing her absolutely pearl-white teeth. There had been a time when Christine would have invariably laughed faced with her deformed reflection. But now she's much too anxious and closes her eyes after passing the mirror, trying to piece her real face, her real body, back together again from the grotesque image.

She doesn't know why it's so important for her to see herself. It's something inside, something that is just beginning to bud, and it's almost painful. After she's walked for a long time on the street, finding only her gray reflection in the shop windows or her deformed face in the rearview mirrors of cars, she looks for a mirror, a real mirror, no matter where – in the entrance hall of a building, in the restroom of a café, in front of a beauty parlor. She goes up to it, stops, stares at herself avidly for a long time, not moving, almost not even breathing, with her eyes glued to the other's, out to infinity.

The sun is invisible on account of the gray clouds, but Christine knows that it must be getting late. Night will be falling soon, not too abruptly; it will creep up along the river valley with the wind. But Christine doesn't want to go back to her place. Her place – that means the apartment with grimy narrow walls, with the greasy smell of food cooking that makes her sick, with the blaring television set, the shouting neighbors, the clattering dishes, all the noises resounding in the cement stairwell, the elevator door creaking and banging from floor to floor. Christine thinks of her father too – her father sitting in front of the television set, stubbled cheeks, hair disheveled; she thinks of her younger sister, her pale face, her eyes with dark circles under them, her sly, ten-year-old-girl ways. She is thinking so intently about her that she screws up her eyebrows and murmurs a few words without really knowing what – an insult maybe or perhaps just like this: "Go away!" She thinks of her mother too, with her tired face, her dyed hair, her heavy limbs and stomach, her heavy silence too, as if there were a mountain of things that had accumulated like so much extra fat.

Christine doesn't really think about all of this, but it crosses her mind, very quickly – images, odors, sounds colliding with one another so rapidly and with such force that for an instant it blots out the surrounding immensity of parking lots and walls with three hundred identical windows aligned. So then she stops, closes her eyes against the great whiteness of this place, against this crust of salt, of snow.

The cold wind starts up again. Directly in front of her, at the foot of the giant building, is the Milk Bar. Christine likes to go there after school, to while away the time before returning to the narrow apartment with her father, her silent mother, and her sister's sly looks. She goes gaily up the steps, pushes open the glass door, and pleasurably sniffs the odor she loves, the odor of vanilla, of coffee, of cigarettes. Today, there's no one in the Milk Bar. Everyone has gone into town or out for a walk by the shore or else for a motorcycle ride in the mountains. The owner of the Milk Bar is all alone, a big man with glasses, sitting behind the counter, reading the newspaper. He's leaning over the paper and reading each line so carefully that he doesn't even notice Christine as she comes in and sits down at a plastic table near the window.

What could he be reading so studiously? But Christine doesn't even think about it; she doesn't care. She loves sitting there, with her elbows on the plastic table, looking out through the window.

Now night is beginning to fall. In the empty street, under the gray sky, darkness creeps slowly up, settles in. From time to time, people walk by and look into the Milk Bar, then continue along their way. Christine would like to know what time it is, but she can't make up her mind to ask the owner, who is still reading his paper word by word, as if he didn't understand what he was reading.

And then Cathie walks past the Milk Bar, and she recognizes Christine. She waves her arms and bursts into the café, speaking so loudly that even the owner wakes up. Cathie is taller and heavier than Christine, with a faceful of freckles and black, frizzy hair. She's older too; she must be about sixteen or seventeen, but Christine manages to look the same age, with her clothes, high heels, and makeup. The owner of the Milk Bar gets up from his stool and comes over to stand before the two girls:

"What will you have?"

"A black coffee," says Cathie.

"And I'll have mine with cream," says Christine.

The owner is still looking at them, waiting for them to say something else. Then he grumbles:

"All right, but I'm closing in ten minutes."

Cathie's always like that: she talks too much, too fast; she gesticulates too much, and it makes Christine a bit giddy, especially because she hasn't eaten anything since morning and she's been walking around outdoors all day long, down empty streets, through town squares, along by the shore. And also Cathie always criticizes everyone; she's truly spiteful, and that too makes your head reel, like a merry-go-round spinning too fast.

Luckily, it's dark out now. Despite his warning, the owner of the Milk Bar doesn't seem to want to close right away. He's still reading the paper but paying less attention, lifting his head regularly to look at the girls. Christine glances over in his direction and catches his shiny-eyed gaze upon her. She blushes and quickly turns her face toward the window.

"Come on!" she suddenly says to Cathie. "Let's go!"

And without waiting, she puts the money for her coffee on the plastic table and goes out. Cathie joins her at the bottom of the stairs.

"What's wrong? Do you want to go home already?"

"No, nothing," says Christine. But now that she's outside, she realizes that she must think about the apartment again, with its dingy walls, with the television babbling to itself, with her father's close-minded face, with her mother's weary body, with that look in her sister's eye.

"Ok, well, so long; I'm going home now," says Cathie. All of a sudden she seems bored. Christine urgently tries to hold her back, putting out her hand.

"Listen, is it – "

But she doesn't know what to say. It's a cold night; the wind is blowing. Cathie pulls up the collar of her blue jacket, gives a little wave, and runs off. Christine watches her go into the apartment building across the way, turn on the time switch. Cathie waits a few minutes in front of a door on the ground floor, then the door opens, closes again. Cathie's gone.

Christine walks a little way down the street, as far as the corner of the parking lot. She leans up against a wall for shelter, in a patch of shadow. The night chill makes her shiver after the fragrant warmth of the Milk Bar. She watches the gray sky, turned pink and luminous in the direction of town, with that dark swath still lingering over the chimneys of the incinerator plant. There's not a sound, or at least no sounds of any importance. Only the dull rumblings of cars and trucks out there on the freeway overpass and the sound of people and children inside the apartments or the nasal voices coming from television sets.

She doesn't want to go back to her parents' place, not yet. She wants to stand still here, leaning against the cold wall, watching the night, the gray, indistinct sky, the great white walls in which hundreds of windows are lit up. And the still cars in the parking lots, splashed with the dappled light of the streetlamps, the trucks parked along the street, the city lights blinking on like tarnished stars. She wants to listen to the jumbled sounds of life in the apartments, listen to them all at the same time, feel the coldness of night. She stands still like that, up against the wall, for a long time, until the cold numbs her legs, her arms, her shoulders. Drops of moisture glisten on her white plastic jacket, on her boots.

And so she starts walking again, through the empty streets, skirting the apartment blocks. She doesn't really know where she's going. First, toward the school building; then she crosses a small playground below street level and walks up the narrow alleys, where little dilapidated houses stand in sparse gardens. Small dogs come yapping against the gates at her, and there are black cats running under the parked cars ahead of her.

When she gets back to the apartment buildings, standing in the middle of their parking lots like giants, she feels the cold, moist light of the streetlamps again, and it makes her shudder.

Then there is the sound of motorcycles rushing toward her. She can hear it erupting between the buildings without knowing exactly where it is coming from. Where should she go? Christine wants to hide because she's standing in the middle of the wide street and because she's exposed by the harsh light of the lamps. She starts running toward the nearest building and flattens her back up against the wall just as the gang of bikers goes speeding down the street. There are six or seven of them, masked with helmets, dressed in black vinyl, with mud-splattered Trial bikes. Christine watches them go around the corner; she listens to the sound of their motors fade away in the distance, die out.

Suddenly she's terror stricken. She doesn't really know what the fear is based on, but it's there inside of her, like a spasm, and it's also all around her – in the silence of the wide, empty streets, the gigantic buildings with their hundreds, their thousands of windows, in the orangey light of the streetlamps, in the cold wind blowing up through the valley, carrying with it the acrid smell of fumes and the rumor of the freeway. It is a strange, vague sort of fear that tightens in Christine's throat, making her hands and back break out in sweat despite the cold.

She walks quickly now, trying not to think of anything. Yet suddenly she remembers the piercing look of the Milk Bar owner, and her heart starts beating faster, as though she could still feel those eyes upon her, spying on her from the shadows. Maybe he really is there. She recalls that he was going to close shop and that he watched her after she went out of the Milk Bar, when she was standing in the street.

And then all of a sudden the bikers are there again. This time she didn't hear them coming. They appeared at the same time as the sound of their bikes. Maybe they had come rolling up in low gear, turning and zigzagging through the lot, slipping between the parked cars to catch her by surprise. Now Christine is standing perfectly still in the parking lot, with the yellow light of the streetlamp shining on her blond hair, on her plastic jacket, on her boots, as the bikes go circling slowly around her. The bikers have their faces masked with the visors of their helmets, and not one of them seems to be looking at her; they are merely circling around her, giving little bursts of their accelerators, making their bikes lunge forward, head and tail lights casting about. As they turn, they narrow the circle down, and now they are passing so close to her that she can feel the heat of the exhaust from their mufflers. Christine stands there, frozen to the spot; her heart is pounding, her legs are wobbly. She glances around at the great buildings, but the walls are so high and there are so many windows lit up, there are so many cars in the vast parking lot, their painted bodies casting a myriad of reflections! The slow, deep sound of the circling motorcycles makes the ground vibrate, makes her whole body vibrate, fills her head. She can feel her legs trembling under her and a sort of dizziness coming over her. Then suddenly, with a cry, she jumps forward and starts running as fast as she can, making a beeline across the parking lot.

But the motorcycles are still behind her; they circle through the stopped cars and come back toward her, blinding her with their headlights, accelerating with short spurts, and the roar of the engines echoes loudly.

Christine doesn't stop. She crosses the parking lot, then runs along the main streets; she hugs the walls of the apartment buildings; she crosses the grounds covered with worn, stubby grass. She runs so fast she can hardly breathe anymore, and the cold wind makes tears stream down her cheeks. From having run so much, she doesn't know where she is anymore; all she can see on all sides are the great white walls of the identical buildings, stretching away into the distance; the hundreds, the thousands of windows; the parking lots spreading out with their parked cars; the streets lit with orange lamps; the scruffy grass on the grounds. Then, just as quickly as they'd come, the motorcycles are gone. Again the heavy silence, the cold, the emptiness grip the high-rise project, and Christine can hear the distant rumor of cars again, out there on the wide bridge crossing the river.

Now she recognizes where she is. Without knowing how, her legs running wildly carried her right up to the building she lives in. She lifts her eyes; she's looking for the windows of the apartment where her father, her mother, and her little sister are. They've already been living there for five months, but she still has to look just as long before she can recognize the three windows right next to the ones with the potted geraniums. The two windows of the large room are lit because that is where her father is sitting in his armchair, eating dinner in front of the television. Christine is very tired now, and the prospect of going back to the narrow apartment, of smelling the greasy odor of food cooking, of hearing the nasal voice of the television almost comforts her.

She climbs the steps, pushes open the door to the entryway, puts her hand on the time switch. Then she sees them. They're there waiting for her, all of them, with their black vinyl jackets and their helmets with the visors drawn down, glimmering in the light of the stairwell.

She can't cry out because something is stuck in her throat, and her legs can't move now. They've stepped up close to her. One of them, a tall one with an aviator jacket and an orange helmet with a tinted Plexiglas visor, comes right up to her; he takes her by the arm. She tries to get away; she opens her mouth; she's going to scream. So then he punches her as hard as he can, with his fist, in the stomach, right in the place where the body bends, and breathing stops. They drag her over to the door by the elevator, and they go down the echoing cement stairs. You can hear the sounds of televisions on the first floor, the clatter of dishes, the cries of children. Underground, the light is gray; it's coming from two or three light bulbs set among the sewage pipes. The bikers are moving quickly; they're dragging Christine's body along, almost carrying her. They aren't saying anything. They open a door. It is a storage room, just barely forty to fifty square feet of space, gray cement, some crates, and on the floor there is an old mattress. They throw Christine to the floor, and one of the bikers lights a candle stuck on an old plate at the back of the compartment. The storage room is so small that they are all standing up against one another. Out in the passageway, the time switch clicks off; now there is only the flickering light from the candle. Christine catches her breath. Tears run down her cheeks, smearing her mascara and her liquid makeup. Her teeth are chattering.

"Get undressed."

The tall one's voice echoes in the narrow compartment, a callous, gravely voice that Christine isn't familiar with. When she doesn't move, he leans over her and yanks at her jacket, tears the collar. Then Christine is afraid; she thinks about her clothing that will be all torn. She takes off her jacket, lays it on the ground. She goes to the other end of the compartment, over by the candle, and takes off her striped sweater; she unzips her boots and slips her pants off, then her panties and bra. She's shivering, naked in the cold basement, looking all raw-boned and scrawny; her teeth are chattering so hard she knows she won't even be able to scream; she's crying a little, whimpering, and the tears further smudge her cheeks with mascara and makeup. Then the boy comes up to her; he unbuckles his belt, pushes her down on the mattress, and lies down on top of her without taking his helmet off. The others crowd around, and she can see their faces looking down at her; she can feel their breath on her skin. Interminably, one after the other, they wrench her open; they tear her apart, and the pain is such that she feels neither fear nor cold, only a wheeling blackness deepening in her, crushing her even farther down than her womb, deeper, as if the wet mattress were falling down a frozen black well, breaking her back. It all lasts for such a long time that she doesn't really know what happened anymore. Every time a boy forces his way inside of her, the pain swells in her body and pulls her down into the well. Hands are smashing her wrists into the floor, pulling her legs apart. Mouths are pressing against her mouth, biting her breasts, stifling her breath. Then the candle sputters even more and drowns in its wax. There is silence, and such terrific cold that Christine curls up in a ball on the mattress; she faints.

When the electric light comes back on, she can see the door of the storage room open and the bikers standing in the passageway. She knows that it's all over with. She gets up, dresses herself, and teeters out of the compartment. Her belly is burning, bleeding; her lips are puffy, swollen. The tears have dried on her cheeks along with the mascara and makeup.

They push her up the cement stairs in front of them. In the entryway, only the tall one hangs back, with his helmet and his aviator jacket. Before going out, he leans over Christine, resting his hand on her neck.

"Bastard!" says Christine, and her voice is trembling with rage and fear. But he presses his hand down on her shoulder.

"If you talk, we'll kill you."

Christine sits down outside on the front steps. She sits there for a long time, not moving, so that the cold will make her impervious, so that the dark night will envelop her and soothe the pain in her abdomen and the soreness of her bruised lips. Then she searches through the parking lot for a parked car with a large rearview mirror on the outside. Slowly, with the diligence of a little girl, she wipes the mascara from her eyes and smoothes out the liquid makeup on her discolored cheeks.

Villa Aurora

A URORA had stood, for all time, up there on the hilltop, half lost in the lush tangle of plants, yet still visible between the trunks of latania and palms, a great, white, cloud-colored palace quivering in the leafy shadows. It was called Villa Aurora even though no name had ever been inscribed on the pillars of the gateway, only a number engraved on a marble plaque that had worn away long before I could ever remember it. Perhaps it had been given the name precisely because of its cloudlike color, so like the faint, iridescent hue of sky at dawn's first break. But everyone knew about Aurora, and it was the first strange house ever shown to me, the first house to etch itself on my memory.

I first heard about the lady of Villa Aurora around that same time, and I suppose she must have been pointed out to me on occasion as she was strolling down the garden paths in her large sun hat or trimming the rose bushes by the wall near the gateway. But my recollection of her is blurred, elusive, barely perceptible, so that I can't be altogether certain of having really seen her at all, and I sometimes wonder if I haven't imagined her instead. I often heard talk of her in conversations (between my grandmother and her friends mostly) that I listened to absentmindedly but in which she quickly stood out as an odd sort of person, a kind of fairy perhaps, whose very name seemed to be filled with mystery and promise: the lady of Villa Aurora. Because of the name, because of the pearly sheen of her house glimpsed through the undergrowth, because of the garden as well – so vast, so forsaken, in which a multitude of birds and stray cats dwelled – whenever I thought of her, whenever I neared her domain, a little adventurous thrill would run through me.

Later on, along with other mischief makers, I learned how to enter that domain through a breach in the old wall, over by the gully on the shady side of the hill. But in those days we no longer talked of the lady of Villa Aurora or even of Villa Aurora itself. We spoke of them in periphrases that we had undoubtedly invented for purposes of exorcising the mystery of early childhood and justifying our trespassing; we would call it "going to the stray cats' garden" or else "going through the hole in the wall." But we were careful to stay in the wild part of the garden, the part where the cats lived, with their miraculous litters of blind kittens, and two or three plaster statues had been given over to the vegetation. During those games of hide-and-seek and reconnaissance expeditions through the jungle of acanthus and bay laurels, very rarely did I glimpse, remote and dreamlike, surrounded by the trunks of palms, the great white house with its fan-shaped stairway. And never once did I hear the voice of the mistress; never once did I see her on the stairs or on the gravel paths or even in a window.

Still, it's strange too when I think about those days – it's as if we all knew she was there, that she lived in the house, that this was her realm. Without even knowing what her real name was, we were aware of her presence; we were her familiars, her neighbors. There was a part of her that dwelled in the place, up there on that hilltop back then. Something that we couldn't really see but that was present in the trees, in the palms, in the shape of the white house, in the two stone pillars of the gateway, and in the high, rusty gate chained shut. It was like the presence of something from olden times, something very gentle and remote, the presence of the old gray olive trees, of the giant, lightning-scarred cedar, of the old walls encircling the place like ramparts. It was also in the odor of the dusty bay laurels, in the clusters of pittospores and orange trees, in the dark rows of the cypresses. Day after day, it was all there, without fail, never changing; and because she was at the core of it all, we were happy, without knowing it, without even intending to be.

We liked the cats a lot too. Sometimes some of the brats would pursue them, throwing stones, but once they were through the breach in the wall, the hunt was off. There in the garden, inside the walls, was the home of the cats, and they knew it. They lived in packs of hundreds, clinging to the rocks on the shady side of the hill or half hidden in the hollows of the old wall, warming themselves in the pale winter sunlight.

I knew them well, all of them, just as if I'd known their names: the one-eyed white tomcat with battle-torn ears, the ginger cat, the black cat with azure eyes, the black and white cat with perpetually dirty paws, the golden-eyed gray she-cat and all her children, the bobtail cat, the tabby cat with a broken nose, the cat that looked like a small tiger, the angora cat, the white she-cat with her three kittens, all white like their mother. They were all famished, terrified, with dilated pupils, their coats grimy or shaggy; and then there were all those bound for death, teary-eyed, runny-nosed, so thin you could see their ribs and backbones through the fur. They all lived in the lovely mysterious garden, as though they were the creatures of the lady of Villa Aurora. For that matter, whenever we would venture near the garden paths, closer to the house, we'd see little piles of food set out on bits of wax paper or on old enamel plates. It was she who fed them, and they alone could approach her, could speak with her. People said she poisoned the food she gave them to put them out of their misery, but I don't think that was true; it was just another story concocted by people who didn't know Aurora and were afraid of her. And so we didn't dare go very near the paths or the walls, as if we belonged to another species, as if we should remain forever strangers.

I loved the birds as well because they were low-flying blackbirds, hopping from tree to tree. They whistled funny, mocking tunes, perched on the topmost branches of the laurels or in the dark crowns of the araucaria. Sometimes I would play at answering them, whistling, because it was the only place that you could hide in the underbrush and whistle like a bird without anyone barging in on you. There were robins too, and every so often near evening time, when darkness was settling upon the garden, a mysterious nightingale would sing his heavenly melody.

There was also something very peculiar in the vast, abandoned garden: it was a kind of circular temple, consisting of tall columns topped with a roof decorated with frescos, and on one side of it was written a mysterious word; it said:

ΟΥΡΑΝΟΣ

I would sit there for a long time, half hidden by the tall weeds, looking through the leaves of the bay laurels at the strange word without understanding. It was a word that took you a long way back, to another time, to another world, like the name of some imaginary land. There was no one in the temple except the blackbirds, which would sometimes hop about on the white marble steps and the wild grasses and vines that gradually overran the columns, entwining them, darkening them in places. In the waning light of dusk there was something even more mysterious about the place; it was due to the play of shadows on the marble steps and to the temple's peristyle, where the magic letters shone out. At the time, I believed the temple was real, and I sometimes went there with other neighborhood children – with Sophie, with Michael, with Lucas – crawling noiselessly through the weeds to contemplate it. But not one of us would have dared to venture onto the steps of the temple for fear of breaking the spell hanging over the place.

Later on – but by then I wasn't going to Aurora's garden any more. Later on someone explained to me what the temple really was, built by some nut who thought he was back in ancient Greece, and even explained the magical word, telling me how to pronounce it – ouranos – and said it meant "heaven" in Greek. He had learned all that in school, and he was certainly very proud of himself, but by then I couldn't have cared less; I mean it was all locked up in my memory already and nothing could change it.

The days were long and bright back then in the garden of Villa Aurora; there was nothing else of any interest in the town or the streets or the hills or even the sea, which we could glimpse off in the distance between the trees and the palms. In winter the garden was dreary and dripping with rain, but it was fine all the same to sit leaning up against a palm tree, for instance, and listen to the drumming of the rain on the great fronds and on the laurel leaves. The air would be still then, frozen, not a bird call or the sound of an insect to be heard. Night fell quickly, heavily, filled with secrets, carrying with it the acrid taste of smoke, and like a breeze blowing over the pond, the damp shadows came rippling through the leaves of the trees over your skin.

Or else, just before summer, the harsh, biting sun would come out amid the high branches, scorching the little clearings near the eucalyptus trees. When the heat was at its peak, I would go slowly, creeping like a cat up to the door in the undergrowth, from where I could see the temple. This was the time when it was most beautiful: the blue, cloudless sky and the white stone of the temple so intense, so dazzling, I would have to shut my eyes. Then I'd look at the magical name, and with only that name, I'd be able to take off, like going to another land, like entering a world that didn't really exist yet. There would be nothing but the blank sky and the white stone, the tall white marble columns, and the chirping sound of summer insects, as though they made up the very sound of the light. I would sit for hours at a time on the threshold of that world, without really wanting to enter it, simply looking at those letters that said the magic word and feeling the power of the light and smells. Even today, I can still recall it, the pungent smell of laurel, of bark, of broken branches baking in the heat of the sun, the smell of the red soil. It's more powerful than reality, and the light that I gathered at that moment in the garden still shines within me more clearly and more intensely than the light of day. Things shouldn't change.

～

After that, there was something like a huge void in my life, up until the time when I just happened to come upon the garden of Villa Aurora again – its wall, its barred gate, the tumble of bushes, the bay laurels, the old palms. Why had I one day stopped going through the breach in the wall, slipping through the brambles and lying in wait for bird calls, for the fleeting shapes of stray cats? It was as though I'd been cut off from childhood, from games, from secrets, from garden paths by some long illness and it had become impossible to make the two ends meet. Where had the child in me gone? For years, he was even totally unaware of being cut off, struck with amnesia, forever banished to another world.

He no longer saw the garden, no longer thought about it. The magical word written on the pediment of the fake temple had been completely erased, wiped out of his memory. It was a meaningless word, simply a word that opened the door to another realm for those who gazed upon it, half hidden in the wall of leaves and branches, still as a lizard in the light. So when you no longer looked at it, when you stopped believing in it, the word would fade, lose its power, and become just like all the other words we look at without seeing – words written on walls, on the pages of newspapers, glittering over shop windows.

It was around this same time that the fellow who studied Greek told me one day, just like that, sort of matter-of-factly, that it meant "heaven," and it just hadn't mattered at all any more. It had become an ordinary subject of conversation, if you know what I mean. Just a subject of conversation, hot air, vacuous.

Even so, I did go out of my way to see it all once again one Saturday afternoon just before exams (that was when I was beginning to study law). I'd left the neighborhood so long ago that I had a hard time finding the street, the one that climbed all the way to the top of the hill, right up to the wall of Villa Aurora. There were tall apartment buildings everywhere now; they'd cropped out in a disorderly fashion on the hillside, right up to its crest, huddling against one another on their great blacktop platforms. Most of the trees had disappeared, except one or two here and there that had probably gone unnoticed in the havoc that had swept over the land: olive trees, eucalyptuses, some orange trees, now lost in the sea of asphalt and concrete, seemed scrawny, drab, aged, on the brink of death.

I walked through the unfamiliar streets, and I was gradually seized with a sense of dread. There was an odd feeling about everything, something like apprehension or maybe a deeply repressed fear, not founded upon anything real, like an intimation of death. The sunlight streamed down over the fronts of the buildings, over the balconies, firing sparks in the vast plate glass windows. The mild autumn wind ruffled the hedge leaves and the foliage of the ornamental plants in the gardens of private residences, for now they were tame plants of garish colors with strange names that I had only recently learned – poinsettias, begonias, strelitzias, jacarandas. From time to time there were still, just like in the old days, mocking blackbirds that screeched after me, that hopped about in the grass of the traffic circles, and the shouts of children and the barking of dogs. But death was underlying everything, and I sensed that it was inevitable. It was coming from all sides at once, welling up from the ground, hanging along the overly wide streets, around the empty crossroads, in the barren gardens, hovering in the gray fronds of the old palms. It was a shadow, a reflection, an odor perhaps, an emptiness that pervaded everything.

So then I stopped walking for a moment to try and understand. Things were so different! The villas had disappeared, or else they had been repainted, enlarged, transformed. In places where there had once been gardens protected by high, moss-grown walls, there now towered vast, intensely white buildings of ten, eight, twelve stories on their grease-stained parking lots. Most disconcerting of all was that I could no longer recall my past. The present reality had suddenly erased all of childhood's memories, leaving only a painful sense of barrenness, of mutilation, a vague, blind anxiety cutting off past feelings from the present. And so, dispossessed, banished, betrayed, or perhaps simply excluded, I sensed an aura of death, an aura of emptiness surrounding the world. The concrete and the asphalt, the high walls, the grass and marigold median strips, the low garden walls with their nickel-plated fencing – all of it had form, was filled with a glimmer of apprehension, was laden with ill will. I had just realized that in straying, in ceasing to keep my gaze intent upon my world, I had betrayed it, had abandoned it to its mutations. I had looked away, and meanwhile things had been able to change.

Where was Aurora now? Hurriedly, I walked along the empty streets toward the crest of the hill. I could see the names of the buildings inscribed in gilt lettering on the marble frontispieces, pretentious and empty names, names tantamount to their facades, their windows, their balconies:

"The Pearl"

"The Golden Age"

"Golden Sun"

"The Resedas"

"Sunnyside Terraces"

I thought then of the magical word, the word that neither I nor anyone else ever pronounced, the word that could only be seen, the word engraved at the top of the fake Greek temple faced with stucco, the word that bore one away into the light, into the raw sky, beyond everything, to a place that didn't exist yet. Perhaps it was that word I'd been missing all these years of my adolescence, years I had spent far from the garden, from Aurora's house, from all the paths. Now my heart was beating faster, and something was oppressing me, bearing down at the very quick of me, a pain, a restlessness, for I knew I wouldn't find what I was seeking, that I would never again find it, that it had been destroyed, devoured.

Everywhere up on top of the hill were gutted gardens, ruins, gaping wounds dug into the earth. At the building sites, tall, threatening cranes loomed motionless, and trucks had left muddy tracks on the pavement. The buildings hadn't finished sprouting up yet. They were still growing larger, biting into the old walls, scraping the earth, unfolding sheets of asphalt, dazzling concrete grounds at their feet.

I squinted my eyes half shut against the light of the setting sun bouncing off all of the white facades. There were no more shadows now, no more secrets. Only the underground garages of the buildings, opening out their wide, black doors, revealing the dark passageways of their foundations.

Every now and then I would think I recognized a house, a wall, or perhaps even a tree, an old laurel that had survived the destruction. But it was like a reflection; it would light up in a flash and then fade away just as suddenly before I could even grasp it; and then all that remained were the desolate surface of the asphalt and the high walls barring the sky.

I wandered around for a long time on the crest of the hill in search of some trace, some clue. Evening began to fall; the light was growing murky and dim; the blackbirds were flying heavily between the buildings in search of a place to sleep. It was they who led me to Villa Aurora. All of a sudden, I saw it. I hadn't recognized it because it was below the level of the circular highway, so crunched down under its supporting wall in the crook of the curve that I saw only its terrace roof and its chimneys. How could I possibly have forgotten it? With my heart pounding, I crossed the highway, running between two cars; I walked up to the wire fence. It was Villa Aurora all right. I'd never seen it up so closely before, and most of all, I'd never imagined what it might look like seen from above, as if from a bridge. Then it struck me as looking sad, gray, forlorn, with its high, close-shuttered windows and the plaster stained with rust and soot, the stucco eaten away with old age and misfortune. It had lost that faint pearly color that had once made it seem ethereal when I spied on it from between the low laurel branches. It had lost its color of dawn. Now it was a lurid whitish-gray, the color of sickness and death, the color of wood in a cellar, and even the soft glow of dusk could not light it.

Yet now there was nothing to conceal or shelter it. The trees around it had vanished, except for two or three dejected, twisted, grimacing olive trees growing under the highway on either side of the old house. Looking closely, I discovered, one by one, each of the old trees – the palms, the eucalyptuses, the laurels, the lemon trees, the rhododendrons – each of the trees that I had known, that had been as close to me as human beings, something like giant friends whom I wouldn't have dared get very near to. Yes, they were there still; it was true: they existed.

But like Villa Aurora, now they were simply empty forms, shadows, very pale and lightweight, as though they were hollow inside.

I stood there very still by the highway for a long time, looking at the roof of the old house, at the trees, and the bit of garden that was left. Then I was seeing beyond it all, contemplating the image of my childhood, and I tried to make what I had once loved come back to life. It would come and then go, come back again, wavering, unclear, maybe even painful – an image of fervor and elation that burned my eyes and the skin of my face, that made my hands tremble. The twilight vacillated on top of the hill, blanketing the sky, then receding, throw-

ing the ashen clouds into abrupt contrast. The town all around had
suddenly stopped short. The cars were no longer driving along in
their lanes, nor were the trains or the trucks moving on the loops of
the expressways. The highway behind me crossed over what had once
been the garden of Villa Aurora, making a long curve almost suspended in mid-sky. But not a single car passed on the highway, no
one. Before disappearing, the last light of the sun held the world spellbound, in suspense, for a few more minutes. My heart racing, face
burning, I tried as quickly as possible to get back to the world I had
loved; with all my might I tried to make it appear quickly – everything I had been, those hollows in the trees, those tunnels under the
shadowy leaves, and the scent of the moist earth, the crickets' songs,
the secret passageways of wild cats, their dens under the laurels, the
white wall of Villa Aurora, light as a cloud, and most of all the temple,
remote and mysterious as an airborne balloon, with on its front the
word that I could see but that I couldn't read.

For a brief moment, the smell of burning leaves came, and I
thought I was going to be able to go in, that I was going to find the
garden once again and along with the garden, Sophie's face, the voices
of children at play, my body, my arms and my legs, my independence,
my path. But the smell died away; the twilight grew dull as the sun
disappeared behind the clouds clinging to the hilltops. And then, everything came apart. Even the cars began moving again on the highway, taking the curve at high speed, and the sound of their motors
fading into the distance tore me with pain.

I saw the wall of Villa Aurora, so close now that, had it not been for
the wire fence along the highway, I could almost have touched it by
stretching out my arm. I could see every detail of the wall – the
streaked, flaking plaster, the stains of mildew around the drainpipes,
the spatters of tar, the scars left by machines when the highway had
been built. The shutters of the high windows were closed now, but

closed as though they would never again need to be opened, closed in the tight-lidded manner of the blind. On the grounds around the house, weeds had grown amid the gravel, and the beds of acanthus were overflowing everywhere, smothering the woodbine and the old orange trees. There was not a sound; nothing moved in the house. But it wasn't the silence of times past, laden with magic and mystery. It was an oppressive, awkward muteness that tightened in my chest and throat and gave me the urge to flee.

Still, I couldn't bring myself to leave. I walked alongside the fence now, trying to catch the slightest sign of life in the house, the slightest whisper. A little farther on, I saw the old, green-painted gate, the one I had once looked upon with a kind of awe, as if it had been shielding the entrance to a castle. It was the same gate, but the supporting pillars had changed. Now they were on the edge of the highway, two cement pillars already gray with soot. The beautiful number engraved on the marble plaque was no longer there. Everything seemed cramped, sad, shrunken with old age. There was a doorbell button with a name written under it, covered with a piece of grimy plastic. I read the name:

Marie Doucet

It wasn't familiar to me because no one had ever called the old lady anything but the lady of Villa Aurora, but I understood, merely in seeing the name written under the pointless doorbell, that it was the woman I loved, the woman I'd spied on for so long from my hiding places under the laurels without ever really seeing her.

Just to have seen her name, and to have loved it immediately, the handsome name that matched my memories so well, made me rather happy, and the sensation of frustration and alienation I had felt in walking through my old neighborhood nearly disappeared.

For a second, I was tempted to ring the doorbell, without thinking, impulsively, simply to be able to behold the face of the woman I'd loved for so long. But that was impossible. So I left. I walked back down the empty streets, amid the tall buildings with their lighted windows, with their car-filled parking lots. There were no more birds in the sky, and the old stray cats had no place to live now. I too had become a stranger.

~

A year later, I was able to return to the hilltop. I'd thought about it constantly, and despite all the activity and futility of student life, deep down, there was still that feeling of uneasiness in me. Why? I think that ultimately I'd never quite been able to get used to not being what I had been, the child who went through the breach in the wall and who'd found all those hiding places and passageways there in the great wild garden among the cats and the insect calls. It had remained within me, alive deep down inside of me, despite all the wide world that had drawn me away.

Now I knew I could walk up to Villa Aurora, that I would ring the doorbell over Marie Doucet's name, and that I was finally going to be able to enter the white house with its closed shutters.

Oddly enough, now that I had a good reason to call at the villa – what with that extraordinary ad in which Miss Doucet offered a "room for a student (male or female) who will agree to look after the house and protect it" – now, more than ever, I dreaded going there, forcing my way in, entering that strange realm for the first time. What would I say? Would I be able to speak to the lady of Villa Aurora normally, without having my voice waver and my words become jumbled, without my eyes betraying my emotion and especially my memories, the awe and the desire of my childhood? I walked slowly along the streets toward the crest of the hill, not thinking about anything, for fear of giving rise to too many doubts. My eyes stared at insignificant things – the dead leaves in the gutters, the steps of the shortcut scattered with pine needles, the ants, the flies drowsing, the discarded cigarette butts.

When I came up below Villa Aurora, I was again surprised at all the changes. In the last few months, construction on several new buildings had been completed, several new sites had been begun, several old villas demolished, gardens disemboweled.

But above all, it was the highway running its curve around Villa Aurora that filled me with a terrible feeling of emptiness and destitution. Cars slid quickly over the asphalt with a sort of whistling sound, then moved off, disappearing between the tall buildings. Sunlight glittered everywhere – on the all-too-new walls of the buildings, on the black tar, on the hulls of cars.

Where was that fair light of the old days, the light I would catch sight of between the leaves on the face of the fake temple? Even the shadows had changed now: great, dark pools at the foot of residences, geometrical shadows of lampposts and wire fencing, hard shadows of parked cars. I thought then of the faint shadows dancing between the leaves, the shadows of trees intertangling, of old laurels, of palms. All of a sudden I remembered the round splashes that the sun would make shining through the leaves of the trees and the gray clouds of mosquitoes. That was what I was looking for on the barren ground, and my eyes stung with the light. That which had remained deep within me for all these years and which now, in this frightful barrenness, in the glaring light of the present, was creating a sort of veil over my eyes, a light-headedness, a fogginess: the shade of the garden, the soft shadows of trees that heralded the dazzling apparition of the lovely, pearl-colored house, surrounded by its garden, its mysteries, and its cats.

I rang only once, briefly, perhaps secretly hoping to myself that no one would come. But after a moment, the door of the villa opened, and I saw an old woman dressed like a peasant or like a gardener; she was standing in the doorway, her eyes squinting because of the bright light, and she was trying to see me. She didn't ask what I wanted or who I was, so I said between the bars of the gate, speaking loudly, "I'm Gérard Estève; I wrote to you about the ad for the room...."

The old lady continued to look at me without answering, then she smiled a little and said, "Just a minute; I'll go fetch the key; I'm coming ..." with her gentle and weary voice, and I realized that it hadn't been necessary to shout.

I'd never seen the lady of Villa Aurora before, and yet now I knew that this was the way I must have always imagined her. An old lady with a sun-baked face, with white, short-cropped hair, and clothing that had aged along with her, the clothing of a poor woman or a peasant, faded with sun and with time. It was all just like her handsome name, Marie Doucet.

By her side, I walked into Villa Aurora. I was intimidated, and I felt ill at ease because everything was so old, so fragile. I walked slowly into the house, not saying a word, almost holding my breath, with the old lady leading the way. I was going along a dark corridor when the door opened onto the sitting room, bursting with golden light, and through the windows of the French doors I saw the leaves of the trees and the palms motionless in the dazzling light, as though the sun need never fade. And as I entered the large, timeworn room, it seemed to me that the walls opened out infinitely and that the house expanded, spread out over the whole of the hill, obliterating everything around it – the buildings, the roads, the deserted parking lots, the concrete chasms. Then I regained my size of old, the size I never should have lost, my child's proportions, and the old lady of Villa Aurora grew larger, lighted by the walls of her home.

My head was spinning so, I needed to steady myself on an armchair.

"What is it?" asked Marie Doucet. "Are you feeling ill? Would you like some tea?"

I shook my head, a little ashamed of my weakness, but the old lady was already going out of the room, answering herself, "Yes, yes, I just happen to have the water heating; I'll be right back, have a seat there...."

Then we drank the tea in silence. My dizziness had disappeared, but I was still filled with that feeling of boundlessness, and I couldn't say a word. I just listened to the old lady talking, telling all about the adventures of the house, probably the last adventure she was living.

"They've come here; they'll come back, I know it; that's why I wanted a helper – I mean, someone like yourself to help me to – I did want a young lady; I thought that it would be best for her and for myself, but in the end, you know, there were two that came here; they looked over the house, they politely bid me good-bye, and I never saw them again. They were afraid; they didn't want to stay here. I can understand how they felt; even if everything seems calm now, I know that they'll come back; they'll come in the night, and they'll bang on the shutters with their iron bars, and they'll throw rocks and give wild shouts. They've been doing that for years now, to frighten me, you understand, to make me leave here, but where would I go? I've always lived in this house; I wouldn't know where to go; I just couldn't. And then there's the building contractor who comes the very next morning; he rings at the door, just as you did. But you will let him in now; you'll tell him that you're my secretary; you'll tell him – But no, it's no use after all; I know well enough what he wants, and he knows how to get it; it wouldn't change anything. They took the lot for the road, for the school, and then they parceled out what was left; they built apartment buildings. But there's still this house; that's what they're after now, and they won't leave me a moment's rest until they've got it, and what for? To build more, still more. So I know that they'll come back in the night. They say it's the children from the juvenile home; that's what they say. But I know it's not true. It's them, all of them – the architect, the building contractor, the mayor and his deputies, all of them; they've been eyeing and coveting this property for such a long time now. They built the road right there in back; they thought I would leave on that account, but I closed the shutters; I don't open them anymore; I stay on the garden side. . . . I'm so tired; sometimes I think I really should go, leave, let them have the house, so that they can finish their buildings, so that it'll all be over with. But I can't; I wouldn't know where to go, you see; I've lived in this house for so long, this is all I know now. . ."

That was how she spoke, with her soft voice that you could barely hear, and I watched the lovely light that changed imperceptibly in the large room filled with antique furniture because the sun was going down along its arched path in the empty sky. I thought of the old days, when I used to hide in the bushes of the garden, when the town was but a rumor, muffled by the trees at the foot of the hill. A number of times I was tempted to tell her what it was like in the old days, when I played in the garden, entering by the breach in the wall, and how the cats would scurry into the underbrush. I wanted to speak to her of the large, bright patch that would spring up between the palm trees suddenly, radiant, like a cloud, like a feather; I even started to tell her, "I remember, Ma'am; I . . ." But the words were left dangling, and the old lady looked at me calmly, with her clear eyes, and I don't know why, I didn't dare continue. Besides, my childhood memories seemed petty now that the city had eaten into Villa Aurora, for nothing could hide the wound, the pain, the anxiety that reigned here now.

Then abruptly I knew that I couldn't stay in the house. The realization was like a shudder; it came over me all of a sudden. The destructive forces of the town – the cars, the buses, the trucks, the concrete mixers, the cranes, the pneumatic drills, the pulverizers – would all come here sooner or later; they would penetrate the sleeping garden and then the walls of the villa; they would shatter the windows, tear holes in the plaster ceilings, splinter the cane screens, crumble the yellow walls, the floorboards, the doorframes.

When I had grasped that, a feeling of emptiness crept over me. The old lady had stopped talking. She was sitting, there leaning slightly forward over the cup of tea growing cold, and she was watching the dwindling light through the window. Her lips quivered a bit, as though she were going to say something more. But she didn't speak again.

There was so much silence in her and here, in this dying villa. It had been ages since anyone had come. The contractors, the architects, even the deputy mayor, the one who had come with the ruling of expropriation in the interest of the general public before the school and the road had been built – no one came anymore; no one spoke anymore. So now it was the silence that was crushing the old house, killing it.

I don't know how I ended up leaving there. I think I must have slipped away like a coward, like a thief, just as the two young girls looking for an au pair room had fled before. The old lady was left alone in the middle of her big, forlorn house, alone in the large room with flaking plaster walls and amber-colored sunlight. I walked back down the streets, down the avenues, toward the bottom of the hill. The cars sped through the night, headlights bright, taillights fleeing. At the bottom, in the grooves of the boulevards, motors rumbled in unison, their clamor filled with menace and hate. Maybe this evening was the very last evening, when the young boys and girls from the juvenile home, their faces smeared with soot, would go into the sleep-filled garden with their knives and their chains. Or maybe on their motorcycles they would glide along the huge curve that crushed the old villa like the coil of a snake, and in passing, they would throw their empty Coca-Cola bottles on the flat roof, and maybe one of the bottles would be filled with burning gasoline. . . . As I went into the crowd of cars and trucks between the high walls of the buildings, I thought I could hear, off in the distance, the wild cries of the city's thugs bringing down the doors of Villa Aurora one after the other.

Anne's Game

H E CLIMBS into the old Ford to go and meet Anne. When he starts the motor up and pulls out of the garage, he notices his mother standing on the gravel. The old woman is blinking her eyes in the bright noon sun; she's holding her hand up to shield her glasses, as if she were trying to recognize the person driving the car. Yet there was no one but him in the house, and it gives him an odd, sort of sinking feeling in his heart, something very distant, incomprehensible. So he turns his eyes away. The automobile rolls over the gravel in the garden, and the wheels bump onto the pavement. Maybe it's the light that is causing the strange feeling, the light shining on his mother's white hair, on the white wall of the house, on the gravel, like searching, insistent eyes.

As the car moves down the street toward the square, he rolls down the windows and feels the hot air on his face. A dry, hot summer breeze that slips up his sleeve and makes his shirt billow out in back. The tires are making a wet sound on the tar, and it occurs to him that the sun is melting the surface of the road. He quite likes that sound and the summer heat, especially the vast, blindingly blue sky over the mountains.

As he begins to drive up toward the top of the hill, he looks out over the landscape he's so fond of. He knows it well, knows every inch of it at any time of the night or day: every tree, every cranny in the stone, and the roofs of the houses scattered below, their streets like deep faults, their yards, the large gray lots.

He thinks about all of that while the car winds up the avenue, curve after curve, all the way to the top of the hill. The sky is dazzling, and the concrete buildings perched on the slopes are whiter than ever; their walls seem to be baking with hot sun. Anne prefers the sea, the beach, the parasol pines, and the white sails of boats when there's a race on. She doesn't trust the mountains; she says the landscape is too hostile, too dry.

He loves the mountains. Ever since he was a child, he's loved the stones, the gray ravines, the dry underbrush that scratches your legs, the smell of musk and plants that floats up from the crevasses, and, above all, the silence of the wind. He remembers back when he used to go hunting in the autumn with his father on Sundays, walking through the brush, over the plateaus or on the barren flanks of the mountains. He can't recall what his father was like or whether he loved him; the only thing he knows about him is this: the interminable hikes through narrow valley bottoms in the pale dawn light under the blue sky, with the silence of stone on all sides, and then a partridge suddenly taking flight or a rabbit bolting, and in that same instant, one lone shot rumbling out to the very bottom of the valleys, like thunder.

That is what he is thinking about as the powerful automobile rounds the large curve in the road with buildings on either side. The sun flashes for a fraction of a second on each bay window, firing a blinding spark. Below, the sea has grown steely; the waves have stilled, etching a net of fine wrinkles over the resplendent light.

Then a peculiar dizziness comes over him from having delved into his most distant memories. It bores a painful hole deep inside of him, and at the same time he feels relieved, appeased, just like every time he's able to break loose, remember the days when he didn't yet know Anne. His heart is beating hard and fast, and his hands are sweating on the steering wheel. He has to wipe them on his pants, one after the other. He slows down a little, steers the car over to the far right of the road.

Before him, the large avenue is very straight. There isn't much traffic; there never is between noon and two o'clock in the afternoon. A few trucks every now and then, semis coming from Italy, loaded with wood, or else tank trucks filled with gas.

At the end of the avenue there is another curve; from there you can see the chain of mountains standing out hard and clear in the cloudless sky. Then you go into a shady spot just before you reach the path leading up to the Observatory. Antoine knows the road so well that he could almost drive it with his eyes closed; that's what he told Anne one day. But today something is different. It's as if this were the first time he'd come here. Each detail, each tree, electric tower, milestone, each wall, each house looms up with painful clarity as he passes, is engraved deep within him forever. Maybe he's never seen them as he does today, with such feverish intensity. There is fear too, deep in everything. Lines slip by, rapid hedges, telephone poles, embankments cluttered with white papers and broken glass. It's the road that is moving forward, not the car. It's the road that is unrolling about the tight-closed cab of the steel car, throwing out its objects, its images, its memories. He would like to close his eyes; he feels a sort of weariness deep down, but his eyes stay riveted on the road, and his whole body responds automatically to the necessities of driving: slight movements of his arms on the steering wheel, pressure of his right foot on the accelerator, eyes glancing up at the rearview mirror or down toward the dashboard.

He sees the path to the Observatory branching off from the corner of his eye, but his body doesn't react. Or rather it reacts by tensing up, maintaining the painful alertness, the speed, the road, the embankments whipping past behind him. He doesn't want to remember; he doesn't want to, as if it were a bad dream that would return just as he was slipping back into sleep and make him suffer even more.

Yet it comes, in spite of himself. It's the leaves of the trees making the sunlight flicker like a rain of sparks on the windshield. The air outside must be cool and breezy for those who can stop, who can stretch out on the carpet of pine needles and breathe, staring up at the blue sky. The smell of Anne is floating everywhere. He can smell it despite the closed windows in the car, despite the smell of gasoline coming through the hole in the floorboard. He smells the strong, sweet smell, the smell of Anne's hair, the smell of her body. They'd stretched out in the garden of the Observatory to have lunch. He can't remember what they ate anymore – maybe a bowl of salad that Anne fixed with cucumbers and corn; she loved that. They drank some rosé wine; he can remember that much. Anne lit up a cigarette, an American brand; she was always changing brands. But they didn't say much of anything; they hardly spoke to each other in hushed voices, as if they were telling secrets, not anything important, little snatches, half-spoken words that the wind whisked away into the light along with the cigarette smoke. In summer it was the crickets that talked.

Now the road has reached the very top of the mountain. To the left he can see the floors of the valleys, mist-filled, shadowy, like from up in an airplane. There's hardly anyone left on the road at this hour of the day. But he doesn't feel hungry or tired. He knows where he's going, where he must go. He doesn't even need to make an effort to remember. This is the way it all had to happen, exactly like this.

The city has become a gray puddle, with scattered flashes of light spread out in the depths of the valley at the foot of the mountains facing the sea. Maybe they tried to pick out Anne's house down there, lost in the knotted thoroughfares. Or else the insurance building that lit up with blue neon signs at night. Maybe they stretched out again in the little stand of pines on the carpet of hard needles, and he'd tasted her lips there for the first time. He thinks of the delicate taste, the taste of blond tobacco mixed with the air coming from deep in her body, and his heart starts beating faster; his forehead and cheeks break out in a slight sweat. He shouldn't have thought of that; he shouldn't have let that come back; he knows he's going to get sick. He stops the car at the edge of the embankment, not far from the curve with the Agip gas station. He'd never seen it so clearly before: the huge cement canopy supported by three gray pillars strung with signs that are rattling in the gusty wind. A big German shepherd is lying on the ground between the gas pumps. When the car stops, the dog raises his ears but doesn't move.

He struggles out of the car, teetering in the wind. It's not so much to get a breath of fresh air as it is to hear the dog bark, just because he wants to hear something, someone, to stifle the silence spreading within him. Up above the road he sees the rocks and brush of the vast, windswept plateau. He doesn't really know why he stopped the car here, right in front of the plateau. The guys from town take their girls up there at night, after having been out drinking and dancing in the discos. Back when he was in high school, everyone talked about the plateau, telling each other about their adventures with girls. And once even, a guy named Caroni, who had an old 2 cv, invited him to go out to the discos and take two girls up to the plateau afterward to have some fun. He refused, filled with a sort of rage, and the story had gone around the high school, and some of the guys had made fun of him.

Bringing those memories back is like being overwhelmed with dizziness again because it's so removed from Anne; it was another era. Yet because of it, he scrambles up the embankment and starts climbing up to the plateau through the loose stones and brush. He doesn't really know what he's looking for; he leans forward, runs across the deserted plateau. The wind is blowing in heavy gusts, a cold wind causing tears to stream from his eyes. The light is so very beautiful up here, so very harsh. The blue sky is immense, streaked with curious white marks left by the airplanes in the stratosphere.

He follows a narrow sort of path that winds through the brush, leading nowhere. The silence is very dense up here because of the wind, the light, the immense blue sky. He walks along with his body hunched slightly forward. He can feel the thorns of the bushes tearing at his pants; the pungent odor of the maquis is inebriating. This is the place, he thinks; this is it, this is it. . . . This is what? He doesn't know.

His childhood, his adolescence maybe, the realization of what he hadn't dared to do – run through the bushes with a girl and then the two of them tumbling down onto the scorched, fragrant earth among the shrubs that rip their clothing, that make little beads of blood pop out on their skin. Fondle the warm body that shies away, stop the voice with his mouth, drink in the laughter at the back of the throat.

But the plateau is silent and deserted; there's nothing but the wind and the blue sky, the dazzling light. It's as if he were trying to hide from his own shadow. That isn't possible.

He sits down in a small shallow dip in the ground, right where there is a sort of clearing and the red earth is bare. The wind is blowing over him, in gusts stirring the branches of the shrubs, but he doesn't feel it down in the hollow. He feels only the sun burning on his face, on his hands. His legs hurt, and he notices all of a sudden that his pants have been torn, maybe by a bramble, and that the skin on his shins is ripped open. It burns too. He walks for a long time over the plateau without being aware of the time; then he thinks of the days he used to spend in the garigue, walking noiselessly behind his father, on the lookout for a flight of partridges or a bolting rabbit. His father didn't take a dog with him ever, even when he went out hunting alone. He said that dogs made noise and smelled strong and that it scared the game off. It was his mother that had told him that, of course, because he can't even re-member hearing his father pronounce a single word.

He walked along behind him, without making a sound, trying hard to put his feet down in exactly the same place his father had. He was frightened, sometimes so frightened that he trembled and his teeth chattered. He was frightened as if it were him that his father was going to kill with his double-barreled shotgun. But he loved to walk far into the mountains, climb up the rocky slopes, or creep silently along the bottom of a ravine, as if you were hunching your shoulders up around your ears.

It was great. And then his father died. So he didn't go into the mountains anymore ever again. Today is the first time, but this isn't really the mountains because it's a sexual landscape up on the plateau. Everywhere up here, they come in the night. They stop their cars down below on the road by the Agip gas station, and the big German shepherd probably barks, yanking furiously at his chain. They come running up through the brush. There's the excited, perhaps a bit panicked, laughter of the girls that the guys pretend to lose in the brush. They fall to the ground and roll around there, up against the bushes. They tear their clothing on the thorns, and the girls' hair is full of dirt and twigs. In summer, the night is filled with the chirp of crickets; it makes a rasping sound that goes to your head.

That dizziness once again. He gets to his feet, faltering across the maquis. The sound of insects rises in ripples, sometimes out in front of him, very nearby, sometimes far behind him. The hot sun has made sweat break out on his face, all over his body; his shirt is sticking to his back, under his arms. He takes off his suit jacket, holds it bunched up in his right hand like a rag, and it snags and tears on the thorns of the shrubs. Then the wind picks up, cold, almost icy, and he shivers. He wanders around for a long time on the plateau, aimlessly, looking at all the clearings in which the bushes and the red earth bear the marks of bodies from the previous night.

The dizziness is like being caught in a trap, because he knows that this is the only place, up here on the plateau, that Anne's shadow isn't lurking. She can't come here; it is a place that is filled with hatred and violence, a bitter and lonesome place, like the moor over which the old man with his double-barreled shotgun is walking.

Everywhere else, she's there, waiting. Everywhere else, there is her light, her sky, her sun, her trees, her stones. He thinks of the sea, and all of a sudden the dizziness stops, and the violence, the fury, the hatred melt away. He stands there, motionless, facing west, out where the sun is starting to go down. There is the immense city, with rumbling thoroughfares, with flashing lights. There is the deep blue, almost black sea, as hard as metal, silent and infinite.

At a near run, he crosses the whole stretch of plateau, whirring with insects, all the way back to the road. The car is still sitting in the sun, bursts of incandescent light glinting from its black hull.

When he sits down, the heat is suffocating. He opens the window, starts up the motor, throws it into first gear, pulls away. It's a long road now that he knows where he's going. He won't forget again now. The city receding into the distance behind him is as lonely as the cursed windswept plateau. It's a place of hatred, of pleasure, and of fear, which are all one.

There's no house for him back there anymore. The rooms won't have anything to do with him; they squeeze their walls around him; they set traps for him with their wallpaper – spearheads, sheaves of skewers, whorls, angular irisations of platinum nuclei. He had changed hotels every night, like someone being tracked by the police, but it was no use. Every night, every day. In his mother's house things were even more terrifying, and he hadn't been able to sit down and eat for days and days now. She's so old, with her white hair and her washed out blue eyes behind the glasses. The light reflecting on her hair and the lenses of her glasses made his heart jump into his throat, made a painful shudder run up his spine. Was he afraid? No, that wasn't it; it was more like a fear inside of him was spreading outward in long shudders.

Now he's cruising slowly down the road in the bright sun. To his right is the sea, seen as if by a bird, so high up that the waves seem to be stopped in concentric circles around the splash of sun. That's what Anne loves most of all, when nothing comes between her and the horizon and you can see the long curved line upon which the sky rests. She can spend hours sitting on a rock looking at the sea, as still as a fisherman. He told her that one day, and she'd started laughing. She said that she used to go fishing with the boys; she made her own fishhooks out of pins that she stole from her mother. But she'd never caught anything but clumps of kelp.

He's entered the peaceful lands now; he's come back to Anne's realm. His heart has calmed down, and he's not thinking of anything but her. The car leisurely follows the road, the same road that the young woman took exactly one year ago. When she left the Observatory, Anne drove toward Italy to see the sea. It was an exceptionally beautiful day; the sky was immense and blank, the dark blue sea was covered with sparkles, and the mountains blazed in the sun. Anne's car tools along quietly, slowly in the open light. Star-shaped reflections slip over its dark green hood. Maybe she's listening to the radio right now – the Bee Gees, or a Brazilian song that says, *Mulher rendeira!*

But the wind is blowing noisily against the windshield, whistling through the openings in the car. Every now and again there is a semi-trailer struggling up the long incline, and the car passes it easily. The sun is warmer now; the mountains to the west can be glimpsed as the car rounds certain curves, dark still silhouettes standing over the iron gray sea.

Soon dusk will fall. The day has slipped quickly down toward the other end of the horizon, with not a cloud, not a thing to hold back time. It is as if the day has slipped toward the past, dragging the living back to meet the dead. Today is the very same day as one year ago. The dark green car is driving along the hot road, suspended between the sea and the sky. The light expands to make a vast opening, or it spreads out its glittering dome, just like the two wings of an angel.

Nothing can be violent or cruel anymore. That is what she has decided, forever, and she is holding the hand of the man she loves very tightly. He feels her heart beating in his palm, has the taste of her mouth in his, smells the intoxicating odor of her hair, the odor of grass, the odor of flesh. The salty tears run slowly down, painlessly, moistening the corners of his lips.

Then the light grows softer, a little blurred, just like when twilight is nearing. The wind whistles over the windshield, in the tires, making its far-away music. The road leads toward the large curve from where you can see Italy off in the distance, like an island of high mountains under the wing of an airplane.

Anne's dark green car is speeding along toward the curve without seeing it because just then an explosion of light flashes off the cab of a semitrailer; she shuts her eyes for a long time, her hands clinging desperately to the wheel as the car tears through the cement parapet with the sound of ripping metal and plunges toward the ravine. Later the truck driver says, endlessly repeats, uncomprehending, "It dropped like a stone and exploded at the bottom like a ball of fire. Like a ball of fire."

But there's no more violence now. No more stabbing destiny, gnawing in the pit of your stomach, haunting your days and nights. Death can no longer gleam in his mother's too white hair or on the expressionless faces of passersby. Nothing subsists; nothing resists. There's music in the wind, in the light, the sky, murmuring in his ear. It is saying, "Come, you come too. . . ." It marks the roads with its signs, arrows, numbers, diagrams, pointing to the treasure.

In the middle of the curve, you can't miss it. Exactly one year ago today. The cement parapet hasn't even been repaired yet. Some chicken wire has been strung up between two iron posts. The black car smacks into the posts at sixty-five miles an hour; it blows away the wire mesh as though it were merely a net of gauze. For an instant, it hangs suspended in the air, gliding, blazing in the sunlight with the wide-open sky straight out in front of it. Then it dives, falls toward the bottom of the ravine; it drops like a stone, and as it touches the ground, it explodes just like a ball of fire.

The Great Life

E VERYONE calls them Pouce and Poussy; at least that's what their nicknames have been since childhood, and not many people know that their real names are Christèle and Christelle. People call them Pouce and Poussy because they're just like twin sisters and because they're not very tall. To be honest, they're actually short, quite short, and both very dark, with the same strange, child-like face and button nose and nice, shiny black eyes. They're not pretty, not really, because they're too small and a bit too thin as well, with tiny arms and long legs and square shoulders. But there's something charming about them, and everyone likes them, especially when they start laughing, a funny, high-pitched laughter that rings out like tinkling bells. They laugh quite often, almost anyplace – in the bus, in the street, in cafés, whenever they're together. And as a matter of fact, they're almost always together. When one of them is alone (which happens sometimes on account of different classes or when one of them is sick), they don't have fun. They get sad, and you don't hear their laughter.

Some people say that Pouce is taller than Poussy or that Poussy has finer features than Pouce does. That might be so. But the truth is it's very difficult to tell them apart, and surely no one ever could, especially since they dress alike, since they walk and talk alike, since they both have that same kind of laugh, a bit like sleigh bells being shaken.

That's probably how they got the idea of starting out on their great adventure. At the time, they were both working in a garment shop where they sewed buttonholes and put pockets on pants with the label Ohio, USA on the right-hand back pocket. That's what they did for eight hours a day and five days a week, from nine to five, with a twenty-minute break to eat lunch standing by their machine. "This is like prison," Olga, a coworker, would say. But she wouldn't talk very loudly because it was against the rules to talk during working hours. Women who talked, who came to work late, or left their post without permission had to pay a fine to the boss – twenty, sometimes thirty or even fifty francs. There was to be no down time. The workers finished at five sharp in the afternoon, but then they had to put the tools away and clean the machines and carry all the fabric scraps and bits of thread to the back of the workshop and throw them in the waste bin. So in fact they didn't really finish work till half past five. "No one stays on for long," Olga would say. "I've been here for two years; that's because I live nearby. But I won't stay another year." The boss was a short man of around forty, with gray hair, a thick waist, and an open shirt displaying a hairy chest. He thought he was handsome. "You'll see; he's bound to make a pass at you," Olga had said to the girls, and another girl had sneered, "The man's a womanizer, a real pig." Pouce couldn't have cared less. The first time he came walking up to them during working hours, with his hands in his pockets and his chest puffed out in his beige acrylic sports jacket, the two friends hadn't even looked at him. And when he had spoken to them, instead of answering, they'd laughed at him with their tinkling bell-laughter, both of them at the same time, so loudly that all the girls had stopped working to see what was going on. His face had turned a deep red out of anger or spite, and he'd left so quickly that the two sisters were still laughing even after he closed the door of the workshop. "Now he'll really be looking for trouble. He's going to hassle the shit out of you," Olga had announced. But nothing more ever came of it. The foreman, a man named Philippi, had simply supervised the rows where the two sisters worked more closely. As for the boss, he avoided coming anywhere near them again. That laugh of theirs sure was devastating.

At the time, Pouce and Poussy lived in a small, two-room apartment with the woman they called Mama Janine, who was really their adoptive mother. Janine had taken Pouce into her home after the child's mother had died, and not long after that, she had also taken in Poussy, who was a ward of the state. She took care of the two little girls because they were all alone in the world, because she wasn't married and didn't have any children. She worked in a Cali Superette and wasn't dissatisfied with her life. Her only real problem was those girls, who were as inseparable as two sisters – those girls, known to everyone in the building, and even everyone in the neighborhood, as "the two terrors." During the five or six years of their childhood, not a day went by when they weren't together, and most of the time it was in order to make some kind of mischief, play some prank or other. They'd ring all the doorbells, change the name tags around on the mailboxes, draw pictures on the walls with chalk, fashion false cockroaches out of paper and slide them under the doors, or deflate all the bicycle tires. When they were sixteen, they had both been expelled from school because they'd thrown an egg down on the principal's head from up in the gallery and because right in the middle of the class assembly they'd gone into one of those infamous bell-like fits of giggling, which was even more irrepressible on that particular day than usual. So Mama Janine had put them into a vocational school to learn sewing, and they both obtained – one wondered how – their Certificate of Professional Aptitude (CAP) as machine operators. Since then, they'd found work regularly in the garment factories, but it was only to quit a month or two later, inevitably leaving everything in an uproar and nearly devastating the entire outfit.

So that's why, on their nineteenth birthday, they were still working in the Ohio Made in USA factory and on the payroll of the boss, Jacques Rossi. When they'd started working there, Pouce had promised Mama Janine to be reasonable and to behave like an honest working girl, and Poussy had made the same promise. But a few days later, the prisonlike atmosphere of the workshop had gotten the better of their resolutions. War had been declared between Rossi and them. The other girls didn't talk much and went straight home as soon as they finished work because they had a fiancé who came to pick them up in a car to take them out dancing. Pouce and Poussy didn't have a fiancé. They didn't much like being separated, and when they went out with boys, they arranged things so that they could meet up and spend the evening together. No boy could hold up under that. Pouce and Poussy didn't care. They would go down to the café–bar–tobacco shop on the corner near the factory and drink beer together, smoking cigarettes rolled with coarse, black tobacco, telling each other a bunch of stories punctuated with their cascading laughter.

They always told the same story, a neverending story that took them far away from the workshop with its neon bars of light, its corrugated iron roof, its wire-grated windows, the deafening sound of all those machines endlessly sewing on those same pockets, those same buttonholes, those same Ohio Made in USA labels. They would be off already, off on the great adventure that took them around the world to all the countries that you see in the movies: India, Bali, California, the Fiji Islands, the Amazon, Casablanca. Or else to the big cities, where there are magical monuments, fabulous hotels with gardens on the roofs, fountains, and even swimming pools with waves, like in the sea: New York, Rome, Munich, Mexico, Marrakech, Rio de Janeiro. Pouce was the one who could tell the neverending story best because she had read about it all in books and magazines. She knew everything about those cities, those countries: the temperature in winter and in summer, the rainy season, the special foods, the interesting sites, the people. Whatever she didn't know, she would make up, and that was even more fantastic.

Listening to her, Poussy would add details, or else she'd raise objections as if she were correcting flawed memories, rectifying some inaccuracy, or else bringing some exaggerated fact back into perspective. They would launch into the neverending story almost anywhere and at any time of day – during the noon break or even early in the morning while waiting for the bus that took them to the workshop.

Sometimes people would listen, looking a bit surprised, and then they'd shrug their shoulders. François, Pouce's boyfriend, would try to slip in a joke here and there, but after a while he'd go stalking off in exasperation. But Poussy liked for Marc to come over and sit with them at the café–bar–tobacco shop because he could play the game so well. He told incredible stories about sneaking onto the Trans-European Express one night without a ticket. Or else about his living for several days at the Maison de la Radio, eating with the staff, and calling his friends on the telephones in the empty offices. With him, you could tell by the way his eyes shone that the stories he told might have been true, and Poussy just loved listening to him talk. Marc wasn't her boyfriend – he was engaged to a very pretty but somewhat vapid girl named Nicole, whom everyone had nicknamed Minnie for no real reason.

That's how they began talking about the great life. At first they talked about it without even realizing it, just as they used to talk of other trips they would go on – to Ecuador or down the Nile. It was just a game, something to dream about, and so forget the prison of the factory and all the problems with the other girls and with the boss, Rossi. And then, gradually, it began to take shape, and they started talking about it seriously, as if it were a sure thing. They just had to get away; they couldn't stand it anymore. Pouce and Poussy couldn't think of anything else. If they waited, they'd end up like all the others, old and embittered, and at any rate, they never would have any money. And even supposing the boss, Rossi, didn't fire them, they knew they couldn't last much longer now.

So one day they left. It was near the end of March, and it was raining; the city was all gray and grimy. A very fine, cold drizzle was coming down, getting everything damp – your hair, your feet inside of your boots, even the bedsheets.

Instead of going to the shop, the two girls met in front of the train station, huddling under the awning, with a single, first-class, one-way ticket to Monte Carlo. They would really have liked to go to Rome or Venice for starters, but they didn't have enough money. The first-class ticket to Monte Carlo had already eaten up most of their savings.

They'd prepared a postcard for Mama Janine, and they'd written, "We're going on vacation; don't worry. Hugs and kisses." And together, laughing, they put the postcard in the mailbox.

When they found themselves inside the plush train, sitting on the brand new seats covered with gray felt, with the navy blue carpeting under their feet, their hearts began to beat very fast, faster than ever before. Then the train set out. First it lumbered through the ugly outskirts, then clipped along at top speed between the embankments. Pouce and Poussy settled in, leaning right up against the window, and they drank in as much of the countryside as they possibly could, to the point of even forgetting to talk or laugh. It was great to be off at last, just like that, without knowing what the future held, without even knowing whether you'd be coming back at all. They hadn't brought any luggage so as not to alert Mama Janine, just a small travel bag with a few things, and nothing to eat or drink. It was a long trip all the way to Monte Carlo, and they didn't have much money left. But if one of them felt a slight pang of worry from time to time, it was hardly noticeable. Anyway, that was part of the fun. Every once in a while, Pouce stole a glance at Poussy and felt immediately reassured. Poussy never took her eyes off the green scenery rolling backward past the wind-flattened raindrops streaking the window.

It was very warm in the compartment, and the sound of the cables clattering monotonously filled their head, so Pouce had dropped off to sleep while her sister kept watch. After Dijon, they had to be on the lookout for conductors, and Poussy shook Pouce awake. Their plan was simple. They would each go into a different car. The first girl the conductor encountered was to keep the ticket; then she'd bring it back to her friend, and they would pass for one another. The conductor was a young man with a small mustache, and he looked more closely at Pouce's chest than he did at her ticket. When he saw her again, a little further up, he just said, "Are you more comfortable up here?" After that, Pouce and Poussy knew they wouldn't have any problems on their trip.

The train clattered on all day. Then, just as night was falling, Pouce and Poussy caught sight of the Mediterranean for the first time, the great, metallic-colored pools between the clefts in the dark mountains.

"It's beautiful!" Pouce said. Poussy inhaled the cold air blowing in from the open window.

"Look, factories."

The tall chimneys were spitting out flames into the dim twilight. It seemed as if the sea were feeding the fires.

"It's beautiful!" Pouce said. "I'd love to go out there." She was thinking she could walk along the edge of the steely lake, between the tanks and the chimneys. It was lonely out on the seashore. The sky was perfectly pure, the color of water and fire.

After Marseilles, the train shot through the night, all lit up, with reflections blinding the windows. Pouce and Poussy were hungry and thirsty and sleepy. They drew the curtains of the compartment and stretched out on the seat. They had a good fright when the conductor opened the door. But it wasn't the same man, and he merely asked:

"Have you already shown your tickets?"

And he was gone again without waiting for an answer.

Later that night, the train stopped at the station in Nice, and the two girls pulled down the window to look out at the immense dome of wrought iron under which chilly travelers bustled. A cold wind blew through the station, and Pouce and Poussy were pale with fatigue; they were shivering.

Then the train was off again, going more slowly now. At each station they thought that they'd arrived and would lean out to read the names: Beaulieu, Cap d'Ail.

Finally the train stopped in Monte Carlo, and they stepped down onto the platform. It was late, past ten o'clock in the evening. People were looking at them strangely, especially the men, all hunched up in their overcoats. Pouce looked at Poussy as if to say, "Well, what do you think of this, huh?" But they were so tired, they didn't even have the strength to laugh.

In the taxi that drove them to the hotel ("the best hotel with a nice view of the sea and a good restaurant"), they had whispered suggestions to each other about what they would eat. Fish, lobster, shrimp, and champagne; this was no beer-drinking occasion.

After paying for the taxi, there wasn't much left in Poussy's drawstring purse – enough to go to the casino the next day and hand out some good tips. In front of the hotel, Poussy got out first and went over to hide behind some bushes while Pouce went in to get the room ("a double bed with a view of the sea"). A few seconds later, key in hand, it was Poussy who was on her way to see room 410. When she came back down, she announced that she was satisfied, except for the sea view, because you had to go out on the balcony, and the bathroom too, which was a bit small. But Pouce gave her a thump on the back, and they both laughed really hard. They had forgotten about being tired. They were in a hurry to get something to eat. Pouce said that she was just ravenous. They separated to go up to the room, Pouce three minutes ahead of Poussy, who had taken the stairs at the end of the hall. The hotel was full of very chic people – gentlemen in suits and jackets, in light-colored overcoats, scarves, and women in lamé dresses or in white satin pants. The navy blue pants and sweaters of the two girls went unnoticed. When they met up again in the large, white room, they got suddenly very elated. They cheered, even sang whatever popped into their heads, and didn't stop until they lost their voices. Then Pouce went and sat on the balcony, in spite of the cold wind, while Poussy ordered dinner over the telephone. It was too late to order fish or lobster, but she was able to get some hot sandwiches and a bottle of champagne, which the bellboy brought up on a small table with wheels. He didn't even look at Pouce's silhouette outside the window, and when Poussy gave him a good tip, his face lit up. "Good night, Mademoiselle," he had said as he closed the door.

The two friends ate and drank, and the champagne made their heads spin, then all of a sudden gave them a migraine. So then they turned out the light and lay down fully dressed on the large, cool bed. They fell asleep immediately.

The next day and those that followed were like a party. First of all, there was sunrise. At the first stroke of dawn, Pouce got out of bed. She'd go into the bathroom and take a long, very hot shower, enjoying the slightly peppery scent of the brand new bar of yellow soap. After bathing, she also loved to wrap up in the large, white terry cloth bath towel, watching herself in the mirror that hung on the door. Then Pouce would emerge, quivering all over with steam, and she would open the beige curtains to watch the day break. A few seconds later, she'd hear water running in the bathroom, and Poussy would come to join her, half smothered in the pink terry cloth bathrobe. Together they watched the gray, pearl-colored sea growing gradually lighter, as the lovely, pure sky lit up in the east, over by the dark headlands. There wasn't a sound, and the unbroken horizon seemed immense, like the edge of a cliff. Just as the sun was about to appear, flights of gulls would glide out over the sea. They'd go swooping by on the wind, level with the floor on which the girls stood, or even higher up, and that gave you a strange heady feeling, something like being happy.

"It's beautiful . . . ," Pouce said again, and she cuddled up closer to Poussy's bathrobe without taking her eyes off the shining sea.

Later on, each taking a turn, they called up the hotel restaurant to have something to eat brought up on the little table with wheels. They ordered all sorts of things randomly from the menu, pretending to be surprised when they were told that it was too early for lobster à l'américaine, and they always ordered a bottle of champagne. They loved dipping their upper lip into the slender glass and feeling the fizzle of the bubbles stinging their nostrils and the inside of their mouths. The young man came back often now; he was the one who brought up the food and the champagne and the morning papers, folded ceremoniously on top of the little table with wheels. Maybe he enjoyed the generous tips that the girls gave him, or maybe he liked to come and see them because they weren't like the other clients in the hotel; they would laugh and always seemed to be having such a good time.

He had also shown them how to adjust the showerhead and how to work the electric blinds, pushing the button to make the plastic slats pivot. He had brown curly hair and green eyes, and his name was Eric. But even so, they hadn't told him their names because they didn't completely trust him.

The first few days they hadn't done much of anything. During the daytime they'd gone out to walk around in the streets, to window shop, then down by the shore, to the harbor, to see the boats.

"It would be so great to go away," said Pouce.

"You mean sail away on a boat?" Poussy asked.

"Yes, sail off, and go far, far, away.... To Greece or to Turkey or even to Egypt."

And so they walked down the wharves, past the long booms, to pick out the boat they would have liked to sail away on. But it was still winter; the rigging snapped in the cold wind, and the moorings groaned. No one was on the boats.

Finally, they found one that they liked pretty well. It was a big, blue boat with a wooden mast and a cabin hardly bigger than a doghouse. It was named "Cat," and that seemed like a really fine name to them too. They even climbed aboard – Pouce went up front and stretched out along the slender stem, looking down into the dark water, and Poussy stood next to the cabin, making sure no one was coming.

Then it started raining, and they dashed for shelter under the porticos of the closed restaurants. They watched the drops falling into the water of the harbor, talking and laughing. There really wasn't a soul anywhere, or hardly. From time to time, a car would go rolling slowly along on the avenue, heading back up into the city above.

Afterward, the two girls went back to the hotel – first one, then the other, as usual – one taking the elevator, the other the stairs, and they ordered a bunch of things to eat over the telephone: fish, shellfish, fruit, cakes. But they didn't drink champagne anymore because it really gave them a terrible headache. They ordered lemon soda or fruit juices or Coca-Cola.

Those were the first couple of days. After that, Pouce grew tired of eating in the hotel room and hiding in the bathroom every time someone knocked at the door for fear it wouldn't be the same bellboy. For that matter, they were both tired of the hotel, and people were starting to look at them strangely – maybe because they were always wearing the same clothes – and there were also people who had seen them together, and Poussy said that they'd end up getting caught.

One beautiful sunny morning, they left – first one, then the other. Poussy went out first, as if she were going out after breakfast for a walk in the garden, by the pool. Pouce threw the travel bag containing their belongings down from the window, and a few minutes later, she went downstairs in turn and stepped out onto the avenue; at the end of the block she met Poussy with the bag. They walked along, talking and laughing, and, since they hardly had any money left, decided to hitch a ride.

Pouce wanted to head for Nice and Poussy for Italy; so they flipped a coin, and Poussy won. Before leaving, Pouce wanted to at least call home to say that everything was fine. She put a coin in the telephone, and when Mama Janine picked up the phone on the other end, she said very quickly, just before the line cut off:

"It's Christèle. Everything's fine; don't worry. Love you."

Poussy said that it surely wasn't worthwhile to make such a short telephone call and that, moreover, Mama Janine might think that they'd been kidnapped and had been forced to talk very quickly.

"You really think so?" said Pouce. It seemed to bother her for a minute, and then she didn't think about it anymore. Later on, Poussy said, "We'll send her a postcard from Monte Carlo. By the time it gets there, we'll already be in Italy and out of danger."

In a tobacco shop, they picked out a card with a picture of the Rock or the Prince's Palace or something along those lines, and borrowing a ballpoint pen, they both wrote, "See you soon, love and kisses," and they signed it: Christèle, Christelle. They put Mama Janine's address on it and slipped it into a mailbox.

They stood at a traffic light on the seafront avenue to hitchhike. It was a beautiful day, and they didn't wait long. A Mercedes stopped, driven by a man of about fifty, dressed like a playboy and smelling of soap. Pouce climbed into the back of the car, and Poussy took the seat beside the driver.

"Where are you going?"

"To Italy," said Pouce.

The man touched the bridge of his sunglasses.

"I'm going only as far as Menton. But Italy isn't far from there."

He was driving fast, and it was making Poussy a little nauseous. Or maybe it was the smell of the soap. He would glance sideways at the girl from time to time.

"Are you twins?"

"Yes," said Poussy.

"It's easy to see," said the man. "You look exactly alike, like two peas in a pod."

He was getting irritated because the two girls weren't in the mood for talking. So he lit up a cigarette. He was passing other cars recklessly, in the curves, and would honk the horn furiously when someone wouldn't let him pass.

Then he said, all of a sudden:

"Do you know it's dangerous for two pretty girls like you to be hitchhiking?"

"Oh really?" Poussy said.

The man gave a little throaty laugh.

"Yes, because if I took you on a little ride to some deserted place, what would you be able to do about it?"

"We know how to look after ourselves pretty well, you know."

The man slowed down.

"What would you do?"

After having thought it over, Poussy said calmly:

"Well, I'd smash you in the Adam's apple with my forearm – it's really quite painful; in the meantime, my friend here would be clapping you over both ears to burst your eardrums. And if that wasn't enough, I'd give you a good jab right in the private parts with a pin I have just for such occasions."

For a little while, the man kept on driving without saying anything; Poussy could see he was having difficulty swallowing. Then the car entered the city of Menton, and the man slammed on the brakes without warning. He leaned over Poussy, opened the door, and said in a strangely mean voice:

"All right, here you are now. Get out of my sight."

The two girls stepped out on the sidewalk. The man slammed the car door, and the Mercedes sped down to the end of the street and disappeared.

"What got into him?" asked Poussy.

"I believe you scared him," said Pouce. And they laughed for quite some time over that one.

They decided to just walk for a little while. They crossed the small town, whose streets were bright with sunshine. In a grocery store, while Poussy asked the shopkeeper something, Pouce grabbed two apples and an orange and stuffed them into the travel bag. Farther along, they sat down on the shore to rest while they ate the two apples and the orange. The sea was beautiful with the cold wind blowing over it – a deep blue, skirted with foam. It was great just sitting there looking at it, not saying anything, biting into the green apples. You forgot about everyone and became very distant, like an island lost out at sea. That was what Poussy was thinking about, about that: how easy it was to go off and forget about people, places, to be new again. It was because of the sun, the wind, and the sea.

The white birds were hovering over the waves, giving out plaintive cries. When Pouce threw a piece of orange peel onto the shingle beach, they came flapping down, screeching, then separated and started floating on the wind once again.

"It's nice here," said Pouce.

She turned to look at Poussy. Her handsome, angular face was already tanned from these days of sunshine, and her black hair sparkled with salt and sunlight. Pouce was more on the reddish side, especially her nose, which was starting to peel.

"What if we stayed here for a few days?"

Poussy said:

"Till tomorrow, all right."

They found a hotel on the seafront avenue, an old hotel that was all white with a garden in the back. It wasn't as luxurious as the one in

Monte Carlo, but they decided to get a room for two this time. As she was registering, Poussy asked, "Would you like us to pay right away?" And of course the receptionist said, "Whenever you like; at checkout is more convenient." It built up people's confidence in you. The room was nice and well lighted, and off in the distance, between the palm trees, you could glimpse the thin line of the sea mingling with the sky.

The evening was especially beautiful when the wind stopped, like a bated breath, and the warm yellow light set the pink, white, and ochre houses aglow, and the sharp silhouette of the old town stood out against the pale sky. It was like being at the very end of the world, "like in Venice," Poussy said.

"We will go, won't we? We'll go to Venice later?" Pouce asked, with an almost childlike inflection, and Poussy smiled and hugged her tightly.

Once, after dinner, they climbed up to the top of a hill, following the paths that wound between the villas and the gardens, to watch the sun set behind the town. There were stray cats under the parked cars and atop the walls, watching them, round-eyed. Up on the hill, there was hardly a breath of wind, and the air was balmy and as warm as in summer, heavy with the fragrance of mimosa. It was nice up there; it was a good place for forgetting. Pouce and Poussy sat down on a slope at the very top of the hill, near a small stand of pines. Dogs were barking; they were prisoners in the gardens of the villas. Evening fell very slowly, casting no shadows, simply fading out the colors one by one. It was like ash. It was very soft, with twirls of smoke rising in places and trails of clouds reaching all the way out to the golden, flame-colored horizon. Then, when night had settled in, lights began to flicker on almost everywhere – on the roofs of houses, in the parallelepipeds of the apartment buildings. There were lights out on the sea as well, the red lamps on the jetty, and, perhaps, far out at sea, hardly visible, the lights of a large container ship bound for Genoa.

The girls watched all of the lights coming on, way down below along the coastline, scattered through the hollows in the hills, the patterns the roads made on the slopes. They also watched the headlights of cars, the little yellow points moving forward so slowly, like phosphorescent insects. They were so far away, so small; they didn't seem very important anymore when you looked at them from up here on the hilltop.

"It's nice being up here," whispered Pouce, and she leaned her head against her friend's shoulder as though she were going to fall asleep. But Poussy felt something strange inside, just like when someone is watching you from behind or when you know something bad is going to happen. Her heart was beating very hard and fast; it was throbbing with heavy, painful thuds in her head and throat. And every now and again a shudder would run down her arms, down her back, an odd kind of prickling that knotted up at the back of her neck. It could well have simply been the night chill. But she didn't mention it to Pouce, not wanting to interfere with her reverie. She held her breath, and after a few seconds, it came out with a heavy sigh.

"What's wrong?" asked Pouce.

"Nothing. . . . Come on, let's go," Poussy said, and she started walking down the hill toward town, toward all the lights moving and shining like so many busy insects.

Eating wasn't always an easy matter. The hotel where the girls were staying didn't serve food in the evenings, and when they were hungry, they had to fend for themselves. One evening, they went out for dinner in a big restaurant on the shore, and when the bill came, they disappeared one after the other through the restroom window. It was a narrow opening, but they were very thin, and they didn't have much trouble slipping out, then running almost all the way back to the hotel. The next day, they did the very same thing in a downtown café. They simply stepped out, strolled calmly away, and each disappeared in a different direction. They had arranged to meet down by the harbor, and as usual, they talked and laughed about it all, glad to have gotten away. "If one of us ever gets caught, we hereby solemnly swear that the other will do whatever she can to help her get away," said Pouce. "I swear to it," answered Poussy.

But after that, they had to change towns because it was starting to get too risky. Pouce decided they should change their wardrobe to go to Italy. They left their blue pants and their T-shirts in a department store and walked out in white outfits: Pouce in Bermuda shorts, a pullover, and a nylon jacket, Poussy in a straight skirt and a wool jacket. In the gift department, Poussy picked out a beaded headband with American Indian designs on it for herself, and she chose a couple of ivory-colored plastic bracelets for her friend. And in the shoe department, Pouce and Poussy left their shoes, which were beginning to get a bit worn, in exchange for low-cut, Western-style boots in white vinyl.

Once they had changed outfits, they left for Italy, without even going to pick up their bag at the hotel. That way, there'd be no problem about paying the bill, and anyway the things they had in their bag were hardly worth going out of their way for. "Besides," said Pouce, "it's easier to hitchhike when you've got your hands free." Poussy had held on to the drawstring purse with their ID cards and the bit of money that was left. But Pouce didn't even have a tube of lipstick.

They would have preferred to travel by train, but they no longer had enough money to buy a ticket. So they walked out of town and waved down passing cars; they didn't wait very long. It was an Italian in a white Alfa-Romeo, and as usual, Poussy got in up front and Pouce sat in back. The man was around forty; he had a shadow of beard on his cheeks and very bright blue eyes. He spoke French poorly, and the two girls didn't speak a word of Italian. But they joked around all the same, and every time the man uttered a mixed up bit of a sentence, they would burst out laughing, and he would laugh too.

Just as they were crossing the border, they all became serious again, but they had no problems. The Italian customs officer looked at the girls' ID cards and said something to the driver, and they both howled with laughter. Then they took off again at top speed along the coastal highway, which twisted in and out among the villas and gardens, which ran out along the headlands and around the bays toward Alassio.

They drove into town near the end of the afternoon. The streets and sidewalks were quite crowded, and Vespas whizzed by on the pavement, zigzagging in and out between trolley cars and automobiles, with their shrill motors whining. Pouce and Poussy watched the whole scene in amazement – they had never seen so much agitation, so many people, colors, lights. The man with the Alfa-Romeo parked in a large plaza ringed with arcades and palm trees. He just left his beautiful new car on the spot, paying no attention to the policeman's gesticulations. He pointed out a large café with white linen–covered tables and took the girls over to sit there, right out in the sunshine. The man said something to the waiter, who came back a few minutes later with two huge dishes of ice cream smothered in whipped cream and chocolate sauce. For himself, he had simply ordered a very black coffee in a tiny little cup. The dishes of ice cream made the girls squeal, and they laughed so hard that people in the plaza turned around. But they didn't seem annoyed or even curious; they laughed also at seeing two pretty girls all dressed in white, with copper-colored skin and their hair all frizzy from the sun and the sea, sitting there at the table in front of those two dishes of ice cream that looked like mounds of snow.

They ate all of the ice cream, and after that, they drank a tall glass of cold water. The man looked at his watch and said, "Me vono" several times. Perhaps he was expecting them to leave with him, but Poussy shook her head, pointing out the whole scene to him – the town, the

houses with their arcades, the plaza where Vespas were circling endlessly, like figurines on a merry-go-round – and she didn't say anything, and he understood immediately. But he didn't seem disap-
pointed or angry. He paid the waiter for the ice cream and the coffee,
then he came back and looked at them for a moment, with his blue
eyes shining in his dark face. He leaned down toward them, one after
the other, saying, "Bacio, bacio." Poussy and Pouce kissed him on the
cheek, breathing in for an instant the slightly spicy fragrance of his
skin. Then he walked back over to his Alfa-Romeo and started up the
motor. They watched him drive around the plaza, join in the ballet of
automobiles and Vespas, and disappear down the wide street.

It was getting late, but the two girls weren't in the least concerned
about where they were going to sleep. Since they no longer had any
cumbersome bags, only Poussy's navy blue vinyl purse with draw-
strings, they started sauntering around the town, looking at the
people, the houses, the narrow streets. There were still quite a lot of
people out of doors, more and more people, because for the Italians it
wasn't the end of the day, but a new day that began with the evening.
People were coming out of all the houses – men dressed in black suits
and shiny shoes, women, children; even old people came out into the
street, sometimes dragging a cane chair behind to sit down on the
edge of the sidewalk.

Everyone was talking, calling to one another from one end of the
street to the other, or else they were talking with their car horns and
their Vespas. Some young boys were walking along on either side of
Pouce and Poussy; they were talking too, constantly, taking them by
the arm and leaning toward them, talking about so many things in
their language that it made the girls dizzy.

But it also made them laugh; it was like being drunk – all these
people in the street, the women, the children running around, the first
lights blinking on in the storefronts, the barber shop with a red

leather and chrome chair where a fat man was reclining, his face covered with lather, getting a shave as he watched the street. The boys who were walking with Pouce and Poussy lost interest, went off, and were replaced by two other dark-haired and dark-skinned boys with very white teeth. They tried to speak to the girls in French, in English, then started chattering in Italian again, smoking fake American cigarettes that smelled like dried leaves. Pouce and Poussy went into dress shops or into a shoe shop and tried on dresses and sandals that looked like Roman buskins, ignoring the two boys waiting outside who were waving and making faces at them through the window.

"They get on my nerves," said Pouce.

"Forget it. Don't pay any attention to them," Poussy said.

But it wasn't easy to get any business done with two clowns like those around. People would stop in front of the shop, trying to see inside; there was even a policeman all of a sudden, and Poussy and Pouce felt their hearts speeding up, but he was only there out of curiosity, just like everyone else. Then he began to resent being seen dawdling about, so he came into the shop and said something, and the saleswoman, who spoke French, translated:

"He wants to know if the boys are bothering you."

"Yes. No." said Pouce and Poussy. They felt a little uncomfortable.

But when they came out of the store, the boys had cleared out, and no one else came near them again, as if everyone had heard about the policeman interfering. Near the end of the afternoon, Pouce started dragging her feet and breathing heavily. Poussy glanced over at her and was a little startled to see her looking so pale, in spite of her tan.

"What's wrong?"

Pouce shrugged her shoulders.

"I'm tired.... I'm cold; that's all."

So they started looking for a hotel. But everywhere they went, it was the same story. When they went into the lobby, the people at the reception desk would give them a strange, veiled look, and they would immediately ask Poussy to pay for the night in advance. It was tiresome, and they would have paid well enough, if only they'd had enough money. But Poussy's drawstring purse was almost empty. So then they pretended to have come simply to inquire about accommodations, and Poussy said, "Thank you; we'll call later for reservations." And they left very quickly, for fear that people in the hotel might think of calling the police.

"So what do we do now?" asked Pouce.

They were a bit tired from the crowd, and also they hadn't been able to get a thing in the stores because of the policeman. So then they went back to Partigiani Plaza, and from there they went out onto the beach. It was evening; not a breath of wind blew over the sea. The sky was pink and immense, the color of pearl, and the tall old houses standing in the sand on the shore looked like beached vessels. Never had Pouce and Poussy imagined anything more beautiful.

"Do you think this is what Venice is like?" asked Pouce.

The seabirds were skimming slowly along the surface of the water, skipping lightly over the waves. There was that dark, distant odor, the taste of salt, and that rose-colored light of the sky on the gray water, on the facades, color of old gold.

"I don't ever want to leave here," Pouce added.

They sat down on the sand, right up close to the skirt of foam, to watch the night come.

They slept there on the beach, shielded from the wind and the curious eyes of passersby by an old staircase leading up to a blind door and the hull of an old abandoned skiff. But the sand was soft and fine, and it still held a bit of the golden warmth from the last light of the sun. It was wonderful to sleep outdoors, surrounded by the slow sound of the sea and the strong smell of salt. It was as if they were on the other side of the world, as if everything that they'd ever known before, ever since they were children, had been wiped away, forgotten.

During the night, Poussy awoke; she was cold, and she wasn't sleepy anymore. Without making a sound, she walked across the beach to the sea. The moon was shining in the black sky, shining down upon the waves, making the foam glow very whitely. As far as you could see, there wasn't a soul on the beach. The shapes of the old houses were dark, their shutters closed tightly against the sea breeze.

The girl listened for a long time to the sound of the sea, the long waves collapsing gently on the sand, casting phosphorescent foamy ruffles out toward her feet. At the far end of the bay shone the Capo Mele lighthouse and still further off, the light of Albenza grayed the sky, above the hills.

Poussy would have liked to immerse herself in the dark water filled with sparkling moonlight, but she was cold and a bit frightened too. She merely took off her boots and walked barefoot through the foam. The water was ice cold, insubstantial, like the moonlight in the dark sky.

Afterward, she sat down next to Pouce, who was still sleeping. And for the second time since they'd begun their journey, she could feel an immense void, very much like despair, rending and tearing at her insides. It was so deep, so terrible out here in the night, on the deserted beach, with Pouce's body asleep in the sand and the wind stirring in her hair, with the slow, inexorable sound of the sea and the moonlight; it was so painful that Poussy let out a little moan and curled into a ball.

What was it? Poussy didn't know. It was like being lost thousands of miles away, deep in outer space, with no hope of ever coming back; like being abandoned by everyone and feeling surrounded by death, fear, danger, without knowing how to escape. Maybe it was a nightmare that had remained with her from childhood, long ago, when she would awaken in the night soaked in cold sweat and she would call out, "Mama! Mama!" knowing there was no one who could answer to that name and that nothing could assuage the feeling of anxiety, and especially not Mama Janine's hand, which would come to rest on her arm as she said in a hushed voice, "Here I am; don't be afraid"; but Poussy, with her whole being, right down to the tiniest particles in her body, would silently protest, "It's not true! It's not true!"

Poussy's despair and solitude were so intense in that particular instant that it must have awakened Pouce. She sat up, her face swollen with sleep, her curly hair full of sand and dried seaweed. She said, "What's happening?" with such a funny voice and with such a sleepy expression on her face that Poussy felt her anxiety suddenly melt away, and she burst out laughing. Pouce looked at her without understanding, and she too began to laugh. Pouce ended up thoroughly awake, and the two of them decided to go for a walk on the beach to start the new day.

They went all the way over to the other end of town, walking along by the old apartment buildings that stood on the beach and that looked exactly like the hulks of boats run ashore centuries ago. Sometimes, as they were passing, a dog would start barking somewhere, or else they would glimpse the furtive shadows of rats running over the sand.

They sat down at the end of the beach by the mouth of the river. They lit up an American cigarette and smoked it without saying a word, their eyes fixed on the black horizon and on the shimmering patch of moonlight. The air was hushed now, as it always is just before dawn. But it was cold and damp, and the girls huddled together to keep warmer. Perhaps just at that moment, Poussy thought of swiping a blanket or a parka from a department store. If the thought did cross her mind, it wasn't so much because she was cold, but because Pouce had started coughing that night. There had been the weariness of all those days of traveling – too much sun and too much wind maybe –

and eating whatever they could get hold of, whenever they could, and then that long night on the damp beach, wrapped in the wind and the sea brine. Now Pouce was shivering, and the hand that her friend held in her own was burning up.

"You're not going to get sick, are you?"

"No, I'll be fine in just a little while," Pouce said.

"The sun is going to come up. We'll go sit in a café."

But Pouce's breath was already wheezing, and her voice was gruff.

All the same, they just kept sitting there on the stones at the mouth of the river, watching the horizon and the sky until the first slow increase of day appeared in the east, a gray patch spreading gradually inland. When the sun appeared in the pale, pure sky, the girls went to lie back down on the sand over by the walls of the old houses, and they fell asleep, dreaming perhaps of travels that would never come to an end.

When the sun was well up in the sky, Poussy awoke. On the vast beach, only a few silhouettes of fishermen could be seen off in the distance, busying themselves with their boats or putting the nets out to dry before repairing them. Poussy was beginning to feel hungry and thirsty. She watched Pouce, stretched out beside her, for quite a long while before realizing that she wasn't asleep. Her face was very pale, and her hands were ice cold. But her eyes were shining and disturbingly bright.

"Are you sick?" asked Poussy.

Pouce answered with a groan. She was wheezing more when she breathed than she had been a little while ago. When Poussy took her by the arm to help her sit up, she saw all the little hairs on her skin standing upright, like gooseflesh.

"Listen," said Poussy; "wait here for me. I'm going into town to try and find a suitcase. That way, we can go to a hotel. And then I'll find something for you to eat and drink. Some tea would be good for you, with lemon."

Since Pouce refrained from answering either yes or no, Poussy left right away. She walked along the beach until she came to a street, and she looked for a department store.

Pouce was left alone on the beach, sitting in the sand, leaning up against the old, flaking wall that the morning sun had begun to warm slightly. She was looking straight ahead of her at the sea and the sky, which were all blurry, as if a smoky haze were engulfing her and cutting her off from reality. She was breathing in small little gulps so that she wouldn't feel the pain deep in her lungs. The short, fast breathing was tiring, and a very slow dizziness crept over her. Now the beach was noisy – children shouting, women's voices, men's voices, perhaps even the jumbled echoes of a radio. But Pouce hardly paid any attention to them; they seemed to be coming from the other end of a very long corridor, choppy, deformed, incomprehensible.

"Como ti chiama?"

The sound of the voice startled her. She turned her head and saw a youth standing there, observing her.

"Como ti chiama?" he repeated. His voice was high pitched but not unpleasant. He was looking at the girl questioningly, taking in her copper-colored face; her white clothing, rumpled with the night; her hair matted and full of sand; and her plastic bracelets.

Pouce understood the question, and she pronounced her name, lifting her hand to show him her thumb.

"Pollice?" said the boy. And he began to laugh, and Pouce laughed too, while he repeated:

"Pollice. . . . Pollicino! Pollicino!"

And then he pointed to his chest with his index finger and said:

"Sono Pietropaolo. Pietropaolo."

Pouce repeated his name, and they started laughing again. She had completely forgotten about the pain in her lungs and the feverish chills. She simply felt oddly dizzy – it was the same feeling you get when you go for a long time without food and without sleep, a weakness that's not really unpleasant.

Pietropaolo sat down next to her, with his back against the wall, and he took out an old, crumpled pack of Chesterfields, from which he extracted two bent, almost broken, cigarettes. Pouce took the cigarette. The sweet smoke felt good, at least for the first couple of puffs; then she began to cough so hard that the boy got down on his knees in front of her, looking a bit alarmed.

"It hurts here," said Pouce pointing to her chest.

"Male," said the boy. "E non hai un medicamento p'ciò?"

"No, no." said Pouce.

The coughing had worn her out; small drops of sweat were beading on her forehead, on either side of her nose, and she could feel her heart beating very fast because of the burning deep in her chest.

The sun was high in the sky now, just about at its eleven o'clock place. Pietropaolo and Pouce kept on sitting there, not moving, not speaking, watching the waves tumbling onto the beach.

Then Poussy came back. She was carrying a heavy, waterproof, khaki-colored jacket over her arm and a bottle of beer. She sat down on the sand, panting like someone who had just run a long way. Pouce was leaning up against the wall, her face drawn, eyes bright with fever.

"Who's this?" asked Poussy.

"It's Pietropaolo ..." said Pouce.

The boy smiled broadly.

"Pietropaolo. Ete?"

"Poussy," said Poussy.

"Poussy?"

Pouce meowed to make him understand.

"Ah! Il Gatto! Gattino!"

He started laughing, and the two girls laughed along with him. Together, they drank the beer, wiping off the mouth of the bottle between swallows. Then Poussy showed Pouce the jacket and explained how she'd come by it.

"It's for you. No way to get a suitcase. They're all chained up everywhere. I nearly got pinched with the jacket. I had to run for God knows how long with this thing over my arm and the salesman yelling, 'Ladra! Ladra!' after me. Luckily, he was fat and got winded before I did."

"Ladra! Ladra!" repeated Pietropaolo, and they all burst out laughing.

Poussy helped Pouce into the jacket.

"It's a little big, but it will keep you warm."

"And the beer?" asked Pouce.

"Oh it was in a case in front of a closed shop. I just took it."

They drank some more beer, taking turns, and then Pietropaolo took out his incredibly crumpled pack of Chesterfields and offered it to the two girls.

Pouce shook her head, and Poussy refused too. She said:

"I'm hungry."

The boy looked at her, baffled. So she pointed to her mouth, opening and closing her jaws.

"Ah si. Vorresti mangiare."

He jumped up and disappeared down one of the streets that led to the beach.

They waited for him, not talking or moving, leaning up against the old wall, watching the sea. A cold wind was blowing gustily; there were dark clouds in the sky. Poussy was thinking about all of the things that were so very far away now – the workshop, the gray streets of the outskirts, the dark room, and the kitchen with Mama Janine sitting there – and for the first time in days, it no longer made her anxious to think about all that, but instead it left her feeling somewhat indifferent, as if she had truly decided that she would never again go back to that house. She was watching Pouce out of the corner of her eye – the childish face, the almost obstinate set of the lips, and the rounded forehead, where the wind stirred in her curls. All muffled up in the khaki jacket, Pouce seemed to be feeling warmer; she was breathing more regularly, wheezing less, and her cheeks were less pale. The girl was staring fixedly out at the sea and the sand on the empty beach, as if she'd fallen asleep with her eyes open.

"We're going back," said Poussy quietly, so calmly that Pouce simply turned her head and looked at her in bewilderment.

"We're going to leave now. We're going back," said Poussy again. Pouce said nothing, but she began staring intently at the sea and the beach again. Only this time tears gathered in her eyelashes and then rolled down her cheeks and were swept lightly back with the wind. When Poussy realized that she was crying silently, she hugged her tightly and kissed her, saying:

"It's not only because of that, you know; I might have gotten sick too, but its because – " But she wasn't able to go on because she couldn't think of a good reason.

"I wanted to go all the way to Venice too, and even to Rome, and visit Sicily, and after that, Greece, but not like this, not like this. . . ."

Suddenly, Pouce got angry. She pushed her friend away, and she tried to stand up. She was trembling, and her voice was all gruff.

"Chickenshit! Chickenshit! You're just saying that, but it's really because you're afraid. You're afraid of going to jail; that's it, isn't it?"

Poussy looked at the girl kneeling in the sand, her eyes all bright with tears, her wind-mussed hair, and the overly large parka with the sleeves hanging down over her fingertips.

"I'm saying it because it's true. We can't keep going; we're at the end of the road. We're going back; we can't keep going; we're going back now."

Her voice was very calm, and it made Pouce's anger subside immediately. She sat back down in the sand and let her head fall back against the wall.

Just then, the boy returned. He was carrying a big loaf of bread and a sack of oranges. He squatted down in front of the girls and held the provisions out to them. He had a friendly smile on his face, and his pale eyes shone in his dark face. Poussy took the bread and the oranges and thanked him. They began eating without speaking. The gulls, drawn by the food, circled about their heads, screeching. When she finished eating her orange, Poussy went to wash her hands and face in the sea, scooping a little water and foam up in her hands. She brought some seawater back for Pouce and ran her cool palms over her friend's forehead, over her eyes.

"We're going to leave now," said Poussy. She pointed over to the other end of the beach in the direction of the setting sun. "We're going home now." Pouce stood up too. She was so weak that she needed to lean on Poussy's shoulder to keep from stumbling.

"Dove? Dove?" asked the young boy. His voice was suddenly anxious. He was walking next to the girls, watching their faces intently, like a deaf person trying to read someone's eyes and lips. "Dove? Dove?"

He tripped over a piece of wood protruding from the sand and hopped along grimacing. That made the girls laugh a little. But he wasn't laughing. He said, and his voice cracked because he was beginning to understand:

"Andro. . . . Andro con voi stessi. Per favore, andro . . . accompagnaré voi stessi. . . ."

But when the girls left the beach to start into town, he just stood there on the sand, not moving, arms dangling by his sides, staring after them. Before going down a small deserted street, Poussy turned around to wave to him, and she could see him way off in the distance, so tiny on the white expanse of beach, just standing there as still as a piece of driftwood by the sea. She didn't lift her hand; she and Pouce walked into the dark town amid the sounds of families sitting down to the noon meal.

Out on the road, at a gas station, they found a truck stopped with TIR marked on the outside. Poussy asked the driver if they could ride with him, and after some hesitation he said yes.

A few minutes later, the huge semi was rolling along, headed for France, with Pouce and Poussy half asleep in the cab. The driver wasn't paying any attention to them. He was smoking cigarettes and listening to Italian radio at full volume. When they reached the border, the policemen examined the girls' papers closely. One of them simply said to them, "Come with us." In the room at the police station there was an inspector in plain clothes, a man of about forty, slightly bald, with hard eyes. When they went in, escorted by the uniformed policeman, the man gave a short laugh and said something like, "So these are our two Amazons." Maybe he didn't say "Amazons," but Poussy wasn't really listening. She was watching Pouce's stubborn profile and wasn't thinking about what was going to happen next – about the long hours of waiting in dusty hallways and dark cells. She was thinking only about the day they would be off again, off and away, far, far away, and this time, they would never come back again.

The Runner

WHEN Tartamella stops the motor of the tarpaulined pickup, the sun is rising over the Roïa River. He's pulled to a stop down below the road on the shingle beach by the thin stream of sky-blue water. He lights up a cigarette and hears the men clearing their throats in the back of the truck before climbing down. He shouts at them once again in his gruff voice:

"End of the line! End of the line!"

The men get down one at a time from the back of the pickup, without hurrying, as if they were afraid of moving around too much after the hours spent driving on the highway. There are quite a few of them – eight, ten maybe. Of every nationality – Greek, Turkish, Egyptian, Yugoslavian, Tunisian. Some are tall and thin, some short, some fat; they are dark-haired, red-headed, with green or yellow eyes. They're dressed in all different ways – thick sweaters, winter overcoats, fake aviator jackets, or worn suits and jackets – and they speak all sorts of languages. But Tartamella can easily pick them out at a glance, for they all look alike because of their poverty, their anxious faces, their hunger. Tartamella is standing behind them on the shingle beach. He stares at them; then he looks up at the sky, which is the pale blue color of cold winter dawns. To make the men feel more relaxed, he passes around a package of American cigarettes. They each silently take a cigarette and wait for a light.

Milos doesn't smoke. He's looking at Tartamella as if he were thinking of something else. His gaze is dark, despite his blue eyes and pale face. Tartamella feels uncomfortable with the man's eyes on him, and he hides his discomfort by feigning anger. All of a sudden he says in Italian:

"What's eating you?"

The other man doesn't answer right away, and when Tartamella shrugs his shoulders and turns his back, he says:

"When are we leaving?"

"Right away," says Tartamella. "As soon as the guide gets here."

"The guide?" Milos repeats.

"Yes, the guide. The runner, if you prefer."

Milos goes over and sits down on a rock facing the shingle beach. The other men soon do the same. They form a small group set apart from the tarpaulined pickup and Tartamella, as if they had nothing to do with one another. Tartamella shrugs his shoulders again and climbs back into the truck. He lights up another cigarette and turns on the radio to kill time. It's playing a song by an Afro-American woman with a deep voice, and it sounds a bit strange in this landscape with the dried-up river, the shingle beaches where the squatting men are silently waiting, and the silhouettes of the high, snow-capped mountains at the far end of the valley against the blue winter sky.

The men aren't speaking to one another. How could they? Each of them speaks his own language, the language of the village he left behind, just as he left his family behind, his wife, his children, to try his luck on the other side. Milos thinks of his mother and father, of the house in the village, of the bald mountains. But it's all so far away already that he's not really sure it still exists. He's been wandering around on the roads for such a long time, sleeping on benches in bus stops or else in cheap hotels, clutching the pocket that his Lena had sewn inside his undershirt where he keeps the bundle of money that should get him across the border.

He didn't know it would be Tartamella; no one had mentioned any names. When he arrived at the station with the others coming from Trieste, he planted himself in front of the stairway lit with neon lights. He set his cardboard suitcase down at his feet and waited. The other men had done the same. They each stood waiting without daring to look at the others, for fear they might be border guards.

Then Tartamella came. He got out of his tarpaulined pickup and walked over to the door of the station, lighting up a cigarette.

Since Milos was up front, standing ahead of the others, the fat man spoke to him first.

"Where are you going?"

Milos understands Italian well, but he doesn't like to speak it. He simply said the name: "Francia."

"Are your papers in order?"

That's the way it was supposed to happen; it had all been arranged before he left Trieste, the man who served as a relay at the Café de la Piazza della Libertà, across the street from the bus station, had said, "They'll ask for your papers, you just show your money."

So Milos opened his shirt and took out a bill folded in four that was marked ten thousand. But he didn't hand it over right away.

Now he's sitting on a stone by the river, waiting. The sky is limpid, and the sun has just risen, glowing on the snowy peaks at the far end of the valley first, then gradually lighting up the other mountains. When the sun touches the shingles of the riverbed, they begin to sparkle; Milos loves the early morning light, and though he is exhausted from lack of sleep and the trip from Milan in the back of the pickup, he's happy to be there just as the sun is coming up.

He's a little afraid too. What awaits him on the other side? And what if the police catch him, lock him up in prison; when could he ever get back to Lena and his parents? They say that they kill foreigners sometimes too. It was an Arab that had told him that in French while he was waiting at the station in Milan. He can hardly speak that language, and the Arab spoke with a strange voice that was harsh and gravelly, and his mean eyes gleamed feverishly, so Milos shrugged his shoulders and didn't listen anymore. But deep inside, a feeling of uneasiness grew without his being aware of it. Where is he going now? What will he gain from this adventure? When will he see Lena again, Lena and her topaz eyes?

Now the sun is high in the barren sky. The men are still waiting, sitting on the bank of the Roïa River, not manifesting the slightest impatience. They're used to waiting for hours, for days, ever since they were children. When the sun burns down too hotly despite the winter chill, they simply go and sit a little farther off, under the leaves of a shrunken evergreen oak. They can hear the noise from the highway now, an unbroken roar coming from the bridge farther upstream. But from where they are sitting, the men can't see the cars. They can only hear the sound of the tires and the motors.

Tartamella is waiting also, smoking cigarettes inside the cab of his truck. But he is growing impatient. He checks his watch more and more often, a thick gold wristwatch that shines on his brown arm.

The men don't have watches. Milos used to have one, but he gave it to Lena when he left so that she'd have something to sell if need be. It's all the same to him. He doesn't need to know the time. The sun is enough. Now that he'll be going far away and maybe even never coming back, what difference does time make? He can wait. At the station in Trieste, he spent two days waiting to meet the man who had information about crossing over to the other side. He slept on the benches in the Piazza della Libertà, and on the second day he ate some bread and overripe fruit that tourists had left in the station before departing.

In the train, he'd traveled sitting on the floor and slept with his head pillowed on his cardboard suitcase. At daybreak, he was able to find a seat in one of the compartments. At the station in Milan, he waited again for a few hours, sitting in the tarp-covered pickup because Tartamella said two men were missing.

They all know how to wait. They don't need to smoke or talk. They're hungry, but they refrain from eating because they know they'll need their provisions later. When they get thirsty, they walk over to the stream and drink a few hasty gulps, fearing that someone from the road might see them. When they have to urinate, they walk a few feet away into the brush; then they come back and sit down with the others again. Tartamella doesn't take so many precautions. He stands beside the blue pickup and pees on the white shingles of the beach. Then he eats greedily, biting into and tearing at a huge sandwich with stale bread that he bought at the station in Milan.

The sun makes the shadows creep slowly out over the Roïa River Valley, hour by hour, draining off the last light of day. Already the snow-capped peaks are turning a light gray, and the thin stream running over the shingle beach no longer reflects the blue of the sky.

The men don't move. Maybe they'd wait here on the beach for days, till they died; they're at such a loss for a place to go. Do the hours or the days count when one is dying of hunger? Milos can't stop thinking about Lena; he thinks about her so hard that at times he realizes he's talking out loud, as if she were there next to him. But no one pays any attention. The other men are silent, absorbed in their exhaustion, their hunger, their waiting. The Egyptian who had traveled in the same train as Milos is lying on the ground with his face in the dying light, and you might think he were sleeping if you couldn't see his eyes shining between the lashes.

Then the guide arrives. No one knows his name, and no one budges when he comes. He talks a little with Tartamella and looks at the men waiting on the beach, and he probably says something like, "Are they all here?" because Tartamella nods his head. The guide is a small, wiry, dark-skinned man, with a weather-beaten face; he looks like a mountaineer. He's wearing blue jeans and a dark green hunting jacket. He has on good hiking boots.

"All right, let's go!"

He gives the order in Italian. All the men get up and start walking toward the beach, following a few yards behind the guide. Milos is up front, his cardboard suitcase in hand.

Before driving away, Tartamella collected all the money. Forty thousand liras from each of the travelers, which he put into a black plastic knapsack hanging from his hairy wrist. Then without saying another word, he climbed back into the tarp-covered pickup and left. The truck skidded up the steep bank to the road. Milos turned around to follow him with his eyes, but he was hidden by the trees. The sound of the motor suddenly vanished.

The guide walks hastily along, not waiting for anyone, like someone who's in a hurry to reach his destination. The men stumble over the stones behind him because their strength is waning. The group wades across the river behind the guide. Milos feels the icy water of the torrent wetting his bare feet inside the old shoes. He takes off the shoes and walks as well as he can over the sharp stones. The other men do the same, take off their shoes. The Egyptian has gigantic blue tennis shoes, and that makes the other men laugh a little. One of them is heavily loaded down with an old, bulging flour sack slung over his shoulder, and when he puts his foot on a flat stone, he slips and falls down in a sitting position. That too causes laughter, but Milos sees the man grimace with pain and helps him to his feet.

"Eucharisto," the man says; he's Greek.

The guide has stopped; he's standing on the other bank of the river, watching the men staggering through the water, over the loose shingles on the beach. His tanned face is expressionless, but his voice is impatient. He simply shouts, in French now, "Get a move on! Get a move on!"

The group strikes out again from the other shore, clambers up the riverbank through the brambles. It is dark now; the sun has gone down behind the mountains on the other side of the frontier. It occurs to Milos that maybe over on the other side they're still in the sunlight, and it makes him want to get there even faster.

First they cross a dirt road, then the train track with rusty rails. There is grass growing on the ballast, and the ties are askew. Higher up, on a gray hill, Milos can see the walls of a village; he hears dogs barking on the farms. Instinctively, the men have stopped, for fear of being seen. But the guide keeps climbing through the brush, still shouting, "Get a move on! Get a move on!"

They skirt the first mountain, a lush dark green from the evergreen oaks and the brush. The valley leads north, and near the ruins of an old chapel they find the beginning of a mule path that winds up to the top of the mountain. The group has broken up now; the most surefooted men are higher up near the guide; the slower ones are farther down, inching along the path, carrying their burdens. They've been walking continuously for over an hour now, and suddenly Milos wonders what happened to the Greek. He leaves his cardboard suitcase in a hole in the bushes, hiding it under the branches, and follows the bends back down the path. He passes the men that are lumbering up with closed faces, and no one says a word to him. Far down at the bottom is the Greek, dragging his old flour sack along as best he can; Milos hears him breathing wheezily. Milos heaves the sack onto his shoulder and without saying anything starts back up the path. When he gets to the place where he'd left his suitcase, he pulls it out of the bushes and hands it to the Greek. He lifts the flour sack back up on his shoulder, and they start out again together.

At nightfall they are near a village. The guide is waiting for the men by the roadside. He's smoking a cigarette, and the glowing red tip is as bright as a searchlight. He says to the men, "San Antonio," and he explains to them that he will go up ahead, and when he whistles, they can follow. He says it in Italian and in bad French, but everyone understands.

The minutes drag out in the dark night on the edge of the road. Milos can feel his legs shaking with weariness, and his mouth is so dry that he can't move his tongue. But the night is cold, and he wants to get going again soon to forget the chill.

They hear the guide's signal off in the distance, and they start walking on the paved road. When they pass the village of San Antonio down below, they can see the lights shining in the houses; they can hear the sounds of human beings, the barking of dogs, and they all feel a pang in their hearts because they're thinking of the villages they left, somewhere in Yugoslavia, in Turkey, in Greece, in Tunisia. The guide is not far ahead; he's looking for the path that forks off and leads up to the frontier. The night is pitch black, dense, and the men almost fall, their feet stumbling blindly over the ground. Milos can hear the sound of hoarse breathing; he knows that the Greek is close behind him.

A few kilometers from San Antonio, at a curve in the road, the guide stops in front of a broken down wall. He doesn't say anything, but all the men understand that this is where they are going to camp, sheltered from the wind and the chill of night. Each of them puts down his burden and finds a place to stretch out in the brush, with his head up against the old wall, without even thinking about scorpions. Milos lays his head on the cardboard suitcase and listens to the Greek's wheezy breathing. Then he suddenly falls asleep.

It is the guide that wakes them, first one, then another. It's still the middle of the night, but the moon has come up, magnificent in the crisp winter sky. It is freezing cold, and Milos sees the misty breath coming out of the little man's nostrils like smoke. He gets up and starts to pick up the flour sack, but the Greek is still resting his head upon it. Milos shakes him harder and harder to wake him up, and he realizes that the Greek isn't sleeping. His eyes are open, and he's groaning.

"Come on, get up," Milos says to him in Serbian. Then in French he says, just like the guide, "Get a move on!"

The other man shakes his head, pulls up his pant leg, shows his leg. In the dim light of the moon the man's leg looks swollen, purplish; the pain is making sweat stream down his face. Milos walks over to the guide, who is getting ready to leave; he points to the man lying on his sack.

"He can't get up."

The guide comes over to the Greek, pulls up the pant leg. His face is expressionless. He fishes the forty thousand liras out of his pocket and lays them down next to the Greek. Then he says all the same, "Go to San Antonio in the morning."

The Greek realizes that the journey is over for him, and tears run from his eyes. But he doesn't say anything, maybe because he can't speak a word of anything but Greek.

Milos picks up his cardboard suitcase and walks away without looking at him; he goes over and joins the group that is beginning to follow the mule path up through the brush toward La Roche Longue.

The journey is interminable, and the men are straggled out miles apart along the path. They're leaning forward as they walk along now, carrying their loads, their eyes glued to the rocks that sparkle on the path like glass in the moonlight, not even trying to look at one another, not even trying to figure out where they are. Milos feels hatred welling up in his chest, hatred for everyone, especially for the guide, whom he glimpses from time to time, a lone silhouette in the distance, slipping through the brush like a fleeing animal. Hatred for this world, for these jagged sharp stones, for the bramble bushes that scratch him, for the pungent smell of thyme and topsoil, and for the freezing wind, and it is the hatred that makes him keep walking, in spite of the hunger and the thirst, in spite of the sleepless nights.

When day begins to break, the men have almost reached La Roche Longue at the top of the pass. One after the other, they sit down next to the guide, who is smoking a cigarette, looking out at the floor of the valley, the sky, paling in the East, and the mist rising from the Roïa River. They rest for a little while, and Milos eats something for the first time since the day before, some bread and cheese. The others imitate him, take their provisions out of their bags. The guide keeps smoking without saying anything. Then he points just above them to the sheer walls of La Roche Longue, lit eerily in the first rays of dawn.

He says: "Francia."

Now they are climbing straight up, not taking any trails. They're following the paths of avalanches, past patches of snow clinging to the rocks. The guide climbs effortlessly because his hands are free and he's wearing good shoes, but the men lose their footing, slip, clutch at the scrubs as best they can, tear their clothing. The man ahead of Milos, a Turk maybe, slips on the stones and ruins a shoe; the half torn-off sole hangs down like a sort of tongue. But he doesn't even stop to repair the shoe, just struggles on, and the razor-sharp stones leave deep cuts on the bottom of his foot.

Milos reaches the summit of La Roche Longue breathless, almost at the same time as the guide. When he looks down on the other side, still in shadow, mysterious, unreal like the world at its very beginning, something comes loose inside of him, makes his head reel. Below, there are the ruins of a village, an abandoned farm, terraced groves of black olive trees, and Le Roc d'Ormea, which looks like a reef overhanging a sea of shadows and mist. Milos wishes Lena were here right now so he could show her all of that, just like in the old days; the first time they met, he'd taken her along the shepherd paths of his youth, all the way up to the place they call the Valley of Satan, and he squeezed the delicate hand in his, and he could see the terror and the wonder of the chasm in her wide eyes.

He puts the suitcase on the ground at his feet, squats down on his heels at some distance from the guide. They don't say anything. But for the first time, Milos feels he is communicating with the other man. Even though they aren't looking at one another, it's clear from the way they are both squatting and gazing out over the magnificent landscape that stretches before them.

The light slowly appears on the mountains, glowing first on the peaks and the jagged Roc d'Ormea jutting out over the darkened valleys. Milos can now distinguish the path they'll be following in France, starting from the high rugged crest, then leading southward, skirting the rocky peak, down through the forest of pines and evergreen oaks, toward the bottom of the valleys. Far to the south, beyond Le Roc d'Ormea and the dark green hills, he can see a familiar white mist that signals the presence of the sea. He is looking out over all of that, squatting on his heels not far from the guide, and everything he sees creeps inside of him like words, like thoughts. He knows he must always remember this so that he can tell Lena about it later, so that she too can come. It also means the end of suffering, the end of unfulfilled desires. The fatigue, the lack of sleep, make him slightly delirious, and he waits for the other men to reach the top and sit down around him, looking out in turn. The sound of their voices, their breathing, reaches him, as all of their lips murmur the same word:

"Francia . . . Francia. . . ."

The guide remains sitting there very still for a long time, balanced on his heels, as if he's decided they have the right to contemplate the promised land. Then when the sun appears behind the high mountains, beyond the Roïa River, he gets up and says again, "Get a move on!" And he starts hastily down the slope toward the bottom of the dale. He walks along without looking back, without waiting. Even Milos has a hard time keeping up with him; he stumbles over the rocks that roll underfoot, blinded by the light. Finally they start walking on the path leading around the rocky peak that shines white in the sun. The cold wind begins to blow through the valley; it penetrates the men's worn clothing. At the foot of the slope, the guide is waiting for them by a spring gurgling up between the oak trees and spilling down the path in cascades. One after the other, the men lay their burdens down and take long, slow drinks of the sparkling, icy water. The trees are luxuriant; there are birds singing. Farther on, the guide startles a rabbit that he tries in vain to kill by throwing stones at it. As for the men, they are too dazed to try anything, despite the hunger gnawing at their bellies.

Farther on, the path widens out; it is paved with stones. They slowly cross Le Plan-du-Lion, near the village of Castellar. The first French dogs start barking on the farms, and the men crouch down a little, to hide behind the bushes. But no one is moving on the farms. Maybe they're still asleep, in spite of the lovely morning light. And now, all of a sudden, the village is right before them, perched atop its rocky crag. When the guide has almost reached the chapel, he stops for a minute, then strikes out again at a quick pace. Milos climbs down the slope behind him. The brush opens out. On the wide, black-topped parking lot facing the village is a blue, tarp-covered pickup. Up front in the cab of the truck, Milos sees the burly Tartamella, smoking a cigarette and listening to the radio.

∼

Time goes slowly by, leaden, weighing heavily on every day, every night, in the dark cellar where the men sleep. How long have they been there? They can't remember anymore. Milos thinks that it's been a month, maybe two or three. Maybe it's not months but years? Sometimes the bearded man comes, opens the door to the cellar, calls out some names. He pronounces them however he likes, mutilating them, but each of the men recognizes his name and hurries over to the stairs, emerges above ground level squinting in the sun, unsteady on his feet. The bearded man doesn't say anything else. He takes the men he's chosen off in the tarp-covered blue pickup, or else Tartamella is there again with his thick sweaty face, waiting behind the wheel. Where are they going? The pickup follows the winding road a long way, goes through cities, down vast avenues filled with cars gleaming in the sunlight. It drives past parks, palm-filled gardens, then hugs the shoreline by the fabulously blue sea. Leaning toward the opening in the tarp, the men nudge one another to take turns looking out, with lips pinched tight and hungry eyes. They see life on the outside – beautiful, fast-paced life, bright reflections, people walking around freely in the streets, pretty girls standing in front of shop windows, children running down the sidewalks.

Every day, Milos thinks about Lena; he thinks about her so hard that it is painful. At first he wanted to write, but Tartamella said he couldn't. He says that the police open letters, that they conduct searches to catch illegal immigrants. He says they'll put him and the others in prison and send them all back home. Sometimes Milos dreams of escaping. When the tarpaulined pickup slows down at a red light or when it stops because Tartamella is going to buy cigarettes, Milos draws back the tarp and gazes out with all his might. All his muscles quiver with the desire to leap out, run down the street in the bright daylight, vanish into the crowd. But he has no money, no papers. Tartamella took all of his savings and his identity card – to keep them in a safe place, he said, but Milos knows perfectly well that it is to keep him prisoner, to prevent him from leaving. The pickup takes its load of men to the work site by the sea, a cement quarry hidden in some remote valley where a huge concrete edifice is being built, or else it drops them off in front of a red brick building, a warehouse in the outskirts, where they have to paint, sand, roughcast, nail casing boards, and bolt small steel girders together.

Then the sky is cold and blue overhead, but they feel free again, just like when they'd come up over the mountain pass and started down into the misty valley at dawn the first time. Milos thinks about that. Every night before falling asleep, he dreams of the day he'll reach the mountain pass, holding Lena's soft hand in his, and together they'll look out over the stretch of valleys, the rocky peaks, the pinewoods below, and the smudge of mist showing the place where the sea begins. He dreams of that; he talks to Lena in his head, lying on the moldy mattress on the floor of the cellar. Sleep doesn't allow him to dream for very long, and he never knows what happens next in the dream, when he walks down into the valley holding Lena's hand. Maybe it is the mental image of Tartamella that keeps him from dreaming, and he sinks into a heavy sleep, impervious to the sound of the other men breathing or the rumbling of motors speeding by on the avenue.

How long has it been? Three months, four, maybe five? Milos knows that quite some time has gone by because it is no longer winter. Now the sun beats down at the work sites. The men have cast off their warm clothes, all except for the Tunisian, who keeps his black wool cap and heavy sweater on night and day. Some new men have come. Milos notices them one day at the construction site. He sees them huddling gloomily together under an awning that is used for storing compressors and pneumatic drills. Two days later, he walks across the work site during the noon break and goes up to them. They are from North Africa, dressed even more raggedly than he and the others are, and they have anxious faces, creased with fatigue. Milos goes up to them; he tries to talk to them in French and then in Italian. He says several times:

"Did you come with Tartamella?"

But they don't answer. Maybe they don't understand. They turn their eyes away; their morose faces take on an even more worried, hostile expression. Milos goes back to the other end of the work site. The foreman immediately gives the signal to go back to work, without leaving them time to eat. The next day, when the bearded man calls the roll for those who will be going to the work site, Milos doesn't hear his name. He stays locked in the cellar for three days without going out, and on the fourth day he is taken to another place, surrounded by bleak mountains, where a quarry is being dug. The rain has turned the quarry into a lake of mud, and all day long he uses his shovel to spread out the mountains of mud that the motorized pump spits up. Then when the sun comes back out, he's given a pneumatic drill and put at the foot of the cliff with some other men, and they spend the whole day chipping away at the blinding white rock. At night, they sleep in a metal trailer set up on stones at the entrance to the quarry. The quarry is surrounded by a barbed wire fence with a gate that is padlocked at night. There is also a big German shepherd that runs around the fence on a chain hooked to a metal wire.

Tartamella is never seen up there; neither is the bearded man from the cellar. The men who work in the quarry are all foreigners – North Africans with skin leathered by the sun and the cold, dressed in indescribable rags; they are dismal and silent, and every time Milos tries to engage them in conversation, they turn their faces away without answering. Maybe they just don't understand, or maybe they've grown mute from living in the quarry. The only people that come in from outside are the men who bring the lunch pails for the prisoners, padlock the gate, and hook the dog's chain to the metal wire running along the fence. But they are just as dismal and taciturn as the laborers in the quarry. Maybe they too are prisoners in their trucks and can't escape the role they've been assigned. Sometimes in the evenings, one of the men listens to the radio on an old white plastic transistor that crackles and emits ripples of strange nasal music that no one understands.

Lying on the grimy sleeping bag, with his head propped up against the metal wall of the trailer, Milos listens to the crackling music and thinks of Lena, of the mountains, of the village, his parents, and his friends. But now it is so far away that it's become a sort of dream, blurred and unreal, in which human beings and things can change from one minute to the next. Only Lena's eyes shine out with steady brightness, dark, deep. They stare at him from the other end of space, call to him. Milos thinks of the day that he will finally be able to leave; he thinks of the long journey home, of the money he will bring back for their marriage. But he sinks into an exhausted stupor before he can finish his dream and falls asleep even before he's finished listening to the nasal song on the radio.

That's the way their days go by, prisoners of the white hole of the limestone quarry, surrounded with the din of the pneumatic drills and the stone crusher that turns the rock into gravel for the gardens of suburban houses and for paving roads. Milos doesn't remember how long he's been living there in the sheet metal trailer that smells of sweat, tobacco, and urine, without speaking, without thinking, stopping his stone drilling to eat the lukewarm stew that the truck drivers bring and falling asleep in the evenings aching with weariness. It is only when the cold sets in again, after the blistering summer months, and when the thunderstorms crash on the other side of the mountains that he realizes a whole year has gone by. Then an unbearable fear comes over him, as if he's suddenly discovered that bottomless chasms have been inexorably dug around him on all sides; the fear oppresses him day and night, prevents him from sleeping. It comes over him so abruptly that at first he doesn't understand what is making his legs weak and his throat and chest feel so tight, and he thinks he's sick. But one evening, lying on the sleeping bag in the close darkness of the trailer, listening to the sounds outside of the wind in the rocks and the German shepherd's chain jingling along the barbed wire fence, listening to the regular sounds inside of the men breathing as they sleep and a cigarette sizzling and glowing red intermittently in the night at the other end of the trailer, he suddenly understands: he is afraid of dying right then and there, tomorrow, some day soon; afraid of dying a prisoner in this quarry, without having gone back to Lena, without having seen her again. The fear of death is so great then that he can't hold it in anymore. He clenches his teeth so hard that his temples and the muscles of his neck hurt, and he feels moist tears on his cheeks and lips. He cries out, a muffled cry, like the grunting of a pig or a sick dog; that's what he can't help thinking, and his clenched fists pound at the floor of the trailer, echo on the sheet metal walls. The men have woken up, but they aren't saying anything, sitting up on their sleeping bags in the dark; even the man who is smoking stops puffing on his cigarette. They sit still, listening, not talking, breathing softly, waiting. The fists beat on the sheet metal walls, knock over a bottle or a lunch pail, beat on the floor, harder and harder, faster and faster; then they slow down, grow weary, and all of a sudden there is only the sound of the panting breath mingled with sobs and the enraged barking of the dog running along the fence. Then silence gradually settles back inside the sheet metal trailer. The men lie back down on their sleeping bags, and their wide eyes peer into the impenetrable darkness.

That is the night Milos decides to escape. He doesn't tell the others about it, but the men understand without him knowing it, and they want to come with him. In the morning, when the foreman arrives in the first truck, the men don't stand up. They remain sitting on the ground in the early morning light; they've put on all of their clothing, and their bags are lying next to them. Milos has his cardboard suitcase, with its torn lid, and he is standing because he's the one who is supposed to do the talking. The foreman understands at first glance, and he doesn't get down from the truck. He even leaves the motor running so he can throw it into reverse if things get nasty. When Milos walks up to ask for the money the men are owed, he doesn't answer right away, as if he is thinking it over. Then he speaks in a slightly muffled voice so that only Milos will hear him. He speaks about the contract, which is for two years, and he promises that everyone will be

paid and that he, Milos, can take one of the trucks and become a foreman and go back to live in the city. The men sit there motionless on
their pile of stones with their bundles beside them, as if they were
waiting for a train.

When the foreman realizes they won't get up, he puts the truck in
reverse and suddenly backs up, leaving the gate wide open. Milos
hears the sound of the motor dying away in the valley; then everything falls silent again. The sky is stretched taut, intensely blue, and a
cold wind is blowing. But the men remain sitting outside, not moving,
except to go and get a drink or to urinate now and again. They aren't
talking, and Milos stares at their dark, impassive faces with a mixture
of curiosity, hate, and admiration. The foreman wasn't afraid of him
but of them – them and their desperate strength. They sit there on the
stones all morning long, looking at the wide-open gate, swinging to
and fro and squeaking in the blustery wind. The German shepherd,
like them, is sleeping with his eyes open, lying by the fence.

Then around midday, the truck comes back, and sitting in the cab
with the foreman is the bearded man that Milos had known when he
was in the cellar of the house in the city. He's the one who counts out
the money and gives it to each of the men, in packets of hundred-
franc bills. Milos is given his roll of bills, and when he takes it, the
bearded man simply says, and it's a statement, not a question:

"You're leaving today."

Milos turns his head, looks over toward the men of the quarry. But
they've all disappeared, along with their bundles. Then, on the other
side of the sheds and trailers Milos hears the sound of the compressor
and the high-pitched ring of the pneumatic drills. He's thirsty. He
walks over to the water faucet near the gate and takes a long drink.
Then he grabs the handle of his cardboard suitcase and walks out the
gate without looking back.

The sun is exactly halfway across the sky; it beats down intensely amid all the blue, despite the cold winter wind. Milos walks faster and faster; he's following the road back down toward the sea, toward the big city filled with noise and movement.

He reaches it at nightfall, just when the streetlamps are blinking on, making large pools of light on the asphalt, and the red taillights on the cars are in endless flight at the ends of the avenues. He hasn't been free for so long that his heart is racing painfully, and he can hardly breathe. The noise and the movement in the streets make his head swim, and he feels nauseous, so he sits down on a bench in front of the train station and watches the cars go past. A police van glides slowly by in front of him, and the police officers glance at him inquisitively. Milos is frightened; he starts walking again, with his old cardboard suitcase bumping up against his legs. He goes into a bar lit with neon lights and sits down at the very back, as far away from the door as possible, next to two men who are playing cards. He orders a beer and a sandwich, eating and drinking almost mechanically. When the bar closes, he's on the street again, not knowing where to go. He'd like to go to a hotel to sleep, but he's afraid of the way the night watchmen in the hotels will look at him. He walks down dark avenues, away from the center of town, until he finds a construction site. He settles in there to sleep, lying in the cement dust, with his head on his old suitcase, rolled up in some large pieces of cardboard that he found strewn about. He sleeps, keeping his hand on his chest over the pocket inside his undershirt where his money is hidden.

In the morning, he leaves the construction site before the workers arrive and continues walking around the city, aimlessly, from one street to the next. The shop windows are shining brightly; the cafés, the restaurants, the theater fronts brim giddily. Milos doesn't dare go in anywhere, only into the bakery to buy some thin loaves of hot bread, which he eats in the public squares, surrounded by pigeons and sparrows. He doesn't dare go into the bars anymore to drink a beer because people look at his unshaven face, burnt from so much sun and cold, and his worn clothing, covered with cement dust.

But he stares at them almost avidly, as if he were trying to understand what made them so distant, so indifferent, as if they didn't belong to the same world as he. There are young women who are so beautiful, with pristine faces haloed in blond or black hair, dressed like Amazons, swinging their hips slowly, slipping over the sidewalk like fairies. But they don't see him; they go right past without looking at him, their handsome eyes hidden behind sunglasses or else gazing through him into the distance. He spies on them in the public squares, in the street, in the reflections on the plate glass windows. Then he sees his own whiskered face appear, with his black, matted hair looking like a helmet, and his emaciated features, his feverish, terrifying eyes. He must turn away and flee from himself, just as the young women alone do when they cross over to the other side of the street as soon as they see him coming.

Nights, in the abandoned construction site, he listens to the rumor of the city, the sounds of radio and television sets, the dull rumbling of cars, and the sputtering of motorcycles. One night he awakens with a start. He peers into the night, holding his breath, and sees the silhouettes of men prowling around the site. Maybe they're trying to find him, to kill him and steal his money? So he slips silently from his cardboard pallet, takes his suitcase, and leaves the construction site. When he gets out into the street, he starts running as fast as he can, straight ahead, without looking back. Then he hides behind a wall in a vacant lot that is used as a dump. He spends the night there in the cold air, faded blue in the electric lights, listening to the sounds of rats scurrying around the lot.

So at the break of day, he strikes out across the city and walks as far eastward as he can. When he nears the border, he turns north and searches until he finds the road that first brought him here. Day after day, he walks toward the high pass, eating the bread he bought in the city's bakeries, drinking water from the fountains. Already the sky is bluer, and the smell of forests full of larches renews his strength. He walks along the sharp, stony paths, through the garigue and the ever-green oaks. When there are no more houses, only the tumbled walls of an old farmhouse from time to time or deserted terraced fields, Milos is no longer afraid. He climbs up toward the top of the moun-tain, trudging along in the bright winter sunshine, as if he were climb-ing back toward the beginning of time, back to the place where hatred and despair no longer exist.

Everything is utterly silent; the cold air stings the skin on his face and hands, wrings tears from his eyes. Then all at once, from between the steep rocks, Milos glimpses La Roche Longue against the stark sky, like looking out from a window and seeing eternity. That is where he is going, clambering up over the loose rocks on the slope, hardly breathing, ripping the skin off his hands and knees, dragging his suit-case along as it bashes against the sharp rocks. His body is heavy with exhaustion; there is not enough air, and every time he feels as if he were going to stumble, he says in a loud voice, just like the runner, "Get a move on! Get a move on!" When he reaches the summit, it is evening, and he looks out over the landscape on the other side: the foothills, the village chimneys smoking in the twilight. Down at the very bottom, in the dark break of the earth, a fleecy mist rises along the Roïa River, the river he crossed one year ago, the nearly desiccated river of forgotten days. Despite the icy wind coming from the snowy peaks, he lies down on the edge of the cliff, eyes wide with fatigue, and stares off into the distance, as if somewhere out there, despite the time, despite the silence, Lena's eyes would suddenly blink open un-der his steady gaze.

O Thief, What Is the Life You Lead?

Tell me, how did it all begin?

I don't know; I don't remember; it was so long ago; I can't keep time straight in my mind anymore; it's the life I lead. I was born in Portugal, in Ericeira. Back in those days it was a small, white fishing village overhanging the sea, not far from Lisbon. Then my father had to leave for political reasons, and we settled in France with my mother and my aunt, and I never saw my grandfather again. It was just after the war; I think he died around that same time. But I remember him very well; he was a fisherman; he used to tell me stories, but now I hardly speak Portuguese anymore. After that, I worked as an apprentice mason with my father, and then he died and my mother had to go to work too, and I was hired by a company that renovated old houses; they had a brisk business. In those days, I was like everyone else: I had a job, I was married, I had friends; I never thought about tomorrow; I never thought about sickness; or about accidents; I worked a lot, and money was scarce, but I didn't know how lucky I was.

After that I went into electricity; I was the one who redid the wiring; I installed household appliances, lighting, hooked everything up. I liked it pretty well; it was a good job.   It was so long ago, I sometimes wonder if it was really true, if that was really the way things were, if it wasn't just a dream I used to have back then, when everything was so peaceful and normal – when I went home at seven in the evening, and in opening the door, I felt the warm air of the house, heard the children shouting, my wife's voice, and she came over and kissed me, and I stretched out on the bed before dinner because I was exhausted, and I stared at the patches of shadow that the lampshade made on the ceiling. I didn't think about anything; the future didn't exist back then, nor did the past. I didn't know how lucky I was.

And now?

Ah, everything is different now. The worst part is that it all happened so suddenly, when I lost my job because the company went bankrupt. They say it was because the boss was up to his eyes in debt; he'd mortgaged everything. So one day he took off, without warning; he owed us three months' salary, and he'd just collected a payment on account for a job. They talked about it in the papers, but no one ever saw him again, him or the money. So everyone ended up totally broke; it was like we had all fallen into this big hole. I don't know what happened to the others; I think they went somewhere else; they knew people that could help them out. At first, I thought everything was going to be all right; I thought I'd find work easily, but there wasn't any work because companies hire people that don't have families, foreigners; it's easier to get rid of them when they need to. And I didn't have a CAP (Certificate of Professional Aptitude) in electricity; no one would have given me the same kind of job. So the months went by, and I still couldn't find anything, and it was hard to get enough to eat, to pay for my sons' schooling; my wife couldn't work; she had health problems; we didn't even have money to buy medicine. And then one of my friends who had just gotten married lent me his job, and I went to work in the blast furnaces in Belgium for three months. It was hard, especially since I had to live alone in a hotel, but I made a good bit of money, and I was able to buy a car with it, a small Peugeot van, the one I still have. Back in those days, I'd gotten the notion that I might be able to truck supplies for the construction sites with the van or else pick up vegetables from the market. But after a while things got even harder because I didn't have anything left at all; I'd even lost my welfare benefits. We were all going to starve to death, my wife, my children. That's what finally made up my mind. At first, I told myself that it was just a temporary thing, just long enough to get a little money together, enough to be able to wait it out. Now it's been going on for three years; I know it'll never change.

If it weren't for my wife, the children, I could go away maybe, I don't know, to Canada, to Australia, anywhere, change scenery, change lives....

Do they know?

My children? No, no, they don't know anything; we can't tell them; they're too young; they wouldn't understand that their father's become a thief. At first, I didn't want to tell my wife; I told her that I'd ended up finding a job, that I was a night watchman on the construction sites, but of course she saw everything I brought home – television sets, stereo systems, appliances, or sometimes knickknacks, silverware – because I stored it all in the garage, and she obviously ended up suspecting something. She didn't say anything, but I could tell that she suspected something. What could she say? We were in such a bad way, we had nothing left to lose. It was either that or go out begging in the streets.... She didn't say anything, no, but one day she came into the garage while I was unloading the car and waiting for the buyer. I'd found a good buyer right away, you know; that guy made a bundle without taking any risks. He had an appliance store in town and an antique shop somewhere else too, somewhere around Paris, I think. He bought all the stuff at one-tenth of what it was worth. He paid more for the antiques, but he was picky; he said it really had to be worthwhile because it was risky. One day he refused to buy a clock from me, an old clock, because he told me there were only three or four of the kind in the world, and he'd probably get caught. So I gave the clock to my wife, but she didn't like it; I think she threw it away a few days later. Maybe it scared her. Yeah, so that day while I was unloading the van, she came in; she looked at me, she smiled a little, but I could tell that she was sad way down deep, and I remember it really well; she simply said, "Isn't it dangerous?" I was ashamed, and I answered no and to please go away because the buyer was coming and I didn't want him to see her.   No, I didn't want my children to learn about it; they're too young. They think I have a job like I used to.

Now I tell them that I work nights and that's why I have to go away at night and sleep some during the day.

Do you enjoy this kind of life?

No, at first I didn't enjoy it at all, but now, what can I do?

Do you go out every night?

It depends. It depends on where I'm going. In some neighborhoods, there is no one around in the summertime; in others, everyone leaves in the winter. Sometimes I have to be patient because I know that the chances are I'll get caught, and quite a long time goes by when I don't go – I mean, don't go out. But sometimes we need money at the house – for clothes, for medicine. Or else it's time to pay the rent, the electricity. I have to manage somehow.   I look for the dead.

The dead?

Yeah, you know, you read the newspapers, and when you find out that someone died, someone rich, then you know that on the day of the funeral you can go by their house.

Is that what you generally do?

It depends; there are no set rules. I do certain jobs only at night, if they're in the outskirts, because I know I won't run into any problems. Sometimes I can do a job during the day, around one o'clock in the afternoon. Usually though, I don't like to do it in broad daylight; I wait till nighttime or even early morning – you know, around three or four; that's the best time because there's no one on the streets; even the police are sleeping at that hour. But I never go into a house when someone is home.

How do you know if someone is home?

You can tell right away when you've had some practice, you really can. Dust in front of the door or dead leaves or papers piled up on the mailbox.

Do you go in the front door?

When it's easy to, yeah; I force the lock or I use a fake key. If the lock resists, I try going through a window. I break a pane of glass with my gloves on so I won't leave any prints and also so I won't cut myself.

What about alarms?

If the system is too complicated, I just forget it. But usually they're fairly simple; you can spot them right away; all you have to do is cut the wires.

What's the first thing you take?

You know, when you break into a house like that, a house you've never seen before, you have no idea what you're going to find. You just have to work fast, in case someone has spotted you. So you just take whatever sells well and won't cause any problems – televisions, stereo systems, appliances; or else silverware, knickknacks, as long as they aren't too cumbersome; paintings, vases, statues.

Jewelry?

No, not very often. As a matter of fact, people don't leave their jewelry behind when they go away. Wine's a good bet too; it sells well. And people aren't all that careful about their wine cellars; they don't put safety locks on them, and they don't pay much attention to what they've got. Then you have to load everything up really quick and get going. Luckily I have a car; I couldn't do it without one. Or I'd have to belong to a ring, become a real gangster, you know. But I wouldn't like that because I think those guys do it for pleasure rather than just out of necessity; they're out to get rich; they're always trying to make the most out of it, do a big job, while I just do it for a living so that my wife and kids will have enough to eat, clothes on their backs, so that my kids can get an education, have a real profession one day.   If I found work again tomorrow, I'd stop stealing right away; I could come home in the evenings with an easy mind again; I'd stretch out on the bed before dinner, I'd stare at the patches of shadow on the ceiling without thinking about anything, without thinking of the future, without being afraid of anything....   Now I have the feeling that my life is empty, that there's nothing behind it all, like a movie set. The houses, the people, the cars, I get the feeling that it's all phony and rigged, that one day they're going to tell me that it was all a sham; it doesn't really belong to anyone.   So I go out in the street in the afternoons to stop thinking about all that, and I start walking aimlessly, walking, walking, whether it's raining or shining, and I feel like a stranger, as if I'd just arrived on the train and I didn't know anyone in town, not a soul.

And your friends?

Oh, friends, you know; when you've got problems, when they know you've lost your job and that you're short of money, they're real nice at first, but afterward they're afraid that you'll come and ask them for money, so. . . .   You don't notice in the beginning, and then one day you realize that you never see anyone anymore, that you don't know anyone anymore. . . . Just exactly as if you were a stranger and you'd just arrived on the train.

Do you think everything will go back to the way it was before?

I don't know. . . . Sometimes I think that these are just hard times, that they'll pass, that I'll go back to work, doing masonry or maybe electricity, everything I used to do in the old days. . . . But sometimes too I tell myself that it will never, ever end because rich people have no consideration for the poor, and they couldn't care less; they keep their riches for themselves, closed up in their empty houses, in their safes. And to be able to have anything, even a crumb, you have to break into their houses and take it for yourself.

How does it make you feel to think that you've become a thief?

It does something to me all right; my throat gets all tight, and I feel completely helpless; you know, sometimes I come home in the evening at dinnertime, and it's nothing at all like it used to be; there are just a few cold sandwiches, and I eat in front of the television with the kids, who don't say anything. Then I see my wife looking at me; she's not saying anything either, but she looks so tired; her eyes are sad and gray, and I remember what she said to me, that first time, when she asked me if it wasn't dangerous. I answered no, but it wasn't true because I know very well that one day it's bound to happen; there'll be a problem. Three or four times already, things almost went wrong; people shot at me with rifles. I'm dressed all in black, in a track suit; I've got black gloves and a ski mask on, and luckily they missed me because of that, because they couldn't see me in the dark. But one day, it's bound to happen; it just has to – maybe tonight, maybe tomorrow, who can say? Maybe the police will catch me, and I'll end up spending years in prison, or maybe I won't run fast enough when someone shoots at me, and I'll be dead, dead.   It's her I'm thinking of, my wife, not myself; I'm not worth anything; I'm not important. It's her I'm thinking of, and of my children too; what will become of them, who in the world will ever think of them?   When I was still living in Ericeira, my grandfather took good care of me; I remember a poem he often used to recite to me in a soft singing voice, and I wonder why I remember that particular poem rather than any other; maybe that's what destiny is? Do you understand a little Portuguese? It went like this, listen:

O ladraō! Ladraō!
Que vida e tua?
Comer e beber
Passear pela rua.
Era meia noite
Quando o ladraō veio
Bateu tres pancadas
A'porta do meio.

Yondaland

Any resemblance to events having actually taken place is impossible.

ANNAH is sitting under the pointed arch in the recess of the large window. This is the place she loves most in the whole world. She loves it because from here you have the best view in the world of the sea and the sky, nothing but the sea and the sky, as though the earth and people had ceased to exist. She chose this place because it's completely isolated, so high up, so secret, that no one could find her here. Like the remote nesting ledge of a seabird, clinging to the face of a cliff that seems to float above the world. Annah is very happy to have found this place. So long ago now – two whole years or maybe even more, when her mother had come back from Africa, after her father's death. Peter had stayed below because in those days he was afraid of heights, and she'd begun scaling the stone wall, using the crevices and the jutting ashlars to pull herself up, and that was how she'd made it all the way up to the porticos. She always got a bit dizzy, but at the same time her heart would beat so fast that it gave her a feeling of giddiness that redoubled her strength and pushed her up to the top.

When she got to the top of the wall and felt the ledge of the window under her fingertips, it was so grand! Then she would slip in through the opening and lean her back up against the stone column, sitting cross-legged like an Indian, and look at the sky and the sea as though she had never seen them before: the clear, slightly curved horizon and the dark stretch where the waves seemed to stand still, trimmed with a hem of foam. This was her place up here, her house, where no one else could come. When she came here, Peter would go as far as the foot of the cliff on the seafront and settle himself down in the rocks amid the whins to keep a lookout. Now and again she heard his sharp whistle or else his call, floating up on the wind:

"Yoo-hooo! . . ."

And she answered in the same way, putting her hands up to her mouth like a megaphone:

"Yoo-hooo! . . ."

But they couldn't see each other. When she was up here, in her house, Annah could see nothing but the sky and the sea.

Before her, the sun continued along its course, shining into the back of the alcove, and out on the sea there was that wide pathway that looked like a fiery cascade. That too was grand. Then she didn't think of anything anymore; everything could just fade away. No, she didn't forget, but people and things in the other world weren't so very important here. It was like being a seagull and flying above the rumbling streets of the town, over the great gray houses, over the damp gardens, the schools, and the hospitals.

Annah sometimes thought of her mother, who was sick, in the big hospital up above the town. But when she was here, in her house, atop the deserted escarpment facing seaward, she could think about that without it hurting her. She stared at the blue sky, at the glistening sea; she soaked up the warmth of the sun, which penetrated to the very core of her being, because afterward she would carry it all to her mother in the hospital ward. She held her hand very tightly, and all the light and the color of the sea would seep into her mother's body.

"Are you working hard at school?"

Her mother always asked her that same question. Annah answered "yes" with a nod, squeezing the thin, feverish hand tightly, anxiously searching her mother's face, until that pale smile she knew so well appeared. No one told her that Annah had been skipping school almost every day for the past three months so that she could go and watch the sea and the sky. The little girl's face was the color of burnt toast now, and there was a strange gleam in her eyes.

Peter alone knew where her hiding place was, but he wouldn't have told anyone, even if they beat him. He'd given his word of honor, raising his right hand while holding Annah's palm in his left. Every day after school he ran along by the sea till he reached the rockslide. He darted into the underbrush and waited there a good long while without moving, in case someone should be watching him. Then he whistled between his thumb and forefinger, and the shrill signal echoed in the depths of the old ruined theater. He waited as his heart drummed in his ears. After a moment, he heard Annah's whistle, muted by the wind blowing up on top of the cliff. It was Peter who had taught Annah how to whistle by putting her two fingers between her lips.

It had all started so long ago. Could today possibly be the day that it would all come to an end? Annah is sitting in the recess of the high window, and despite the blazing winter sun, she is trembling and her teeth are chattering nervously. She knows that she's alone. She is utterly alone, and it's as if she were awaiting death. Annah used to think that it wasn't difficult to await death. All you had to do was be indifferent, as hard as a rock, and you could lock out the fear. But today, alone in her hiding place, her whole body is trembling. If only Peter were here. Maybe she would be braver. She tries to whistle, but she's trembling so hard that she can't manage it. And so instead she shouts the signal out:

"Yoo-hooo! ..."

but her call is lost in the wind.

She's straining as hard as she can to hear the moment when the wreckers will arrive. She doesn't know who they are, but she knows they're going to come, now, to tear down the walls of Yondaland.

Annah is listening with all her might. She's listening to the eerie sound of the wind in the metal structures of the large, empty room under the stone archways. She remembers the first time she walked through the abandoned theater. She was walking along the concrete-walled corridor. The darkness was stifling after all the light of the sky and the sea. Farther along, she had gone inside the haunted house; she'd climbed the marble and stucco stairway; stopped in the patio, lighted with a cavelike glow; looked at the crumpled stage sets, the twisted colonnades supporting the shattered stained glass windows, the stone fountain, run dry; and she had shuddered, as though she were the first to violate the secret of this sanctuary. For the very first time, she'd gotten that funny feeling, as though someone were hiding and watching her. At first it frightened her, but it wasn't a hostile look; on the contrary, it was quite gentle, remote, as if in a dream, a gaze that came from all sides at once, enveloped her, permeated her. And so she turned back, guided by the plaintive music of the metal structures on the ceiling of the abandoned theater, knocking against one another in the wind. The slow creaking music gave her the feeling of flying out of doors into the dazzling sky.

Here they come; they're coming now. Already Yondaland is surrounded by fences and barbed wire. They put up all of their signs with frightful words written on them, like orders:

Work Site – Off Limits

Danger

Blasting Zone

They brought in the yellow machines – the crane whose giant arm sways in the wind, the compressors, the bulldozers, and the machine with a huge ball of black metal hanging on the end of its arm. Peter says it's for knocking down walls; he saw one just like it in town; it swings its weight and then hurls itself into the houses, which crumble as if they were made of dust.

The machines have been here for several days now, and Annah is waiting in the house at the top of the escarpment. She knows that if she leaves, the wreckers will start up their machines and will batter down all the walls.

She can hear their voices above her. They enter the realm of Yonda-land from the highway; they cross the terraced gardens, where the brambles and the stray cats dwell. Annah can hear the sound of their boots echoing on the cement roofs, in the corridors of the abandoned theater. She thinks of the fleeing cats, of the lizards stopping short on the edge of their cracks, their throats athrob. Her heart begins to beat harder and faster, and she thinks that she too would like to flee, hide down at the bottom of the cliff, amid the fallen rocks. But she doesn't dare move, for fear the workmen will see her. She curls herself up as tightly as possible at the back of the alcove, doubling her legs up under herself, hiding her hands in the pockets of her parka.

Time goes slowly by when it brings destruction in its wake. By blinking her eyes, Annah can see the sky that she so loves fill with birds, with flies, with spiderwebs. The distant sea is like a sheet of iron – hard, smooth, glossy. A strong wind is blowing, a cold wind chilling the little girl to the bone, clouding her eyes with tears. She's waiting and trembling. She wishes that something would snap, that the big yellow machines would finally get moving, unleashing their jaws, their arms, their rostrums, letting loose their crushing bulk on the old walls. But nothing happens. There is only the thin humming of a mo-tor, very faint, and the sound of pneumatic drills somewhere on the terraces. As the sun reaches its midday point in the winter sky, Annah calls out to her friend once again. She whistles between her fingers and shouts: "Yoo-hooo! . . ."

But no one answers. Maybe they know that he's supposed to come and meet her, and they locked him up in the classroom behind the high walls of the school. Maybe they're questioning him so that he'll tell them everything he knows. But he'd given Annah his word of honor, raising his right hand while holding the little girl's palm in his left, and she knows he won't talk.

The work site falls silent again. It's noon, and the demolition workers are eating their lunch. Or maybe they've gone for good? Annah is so tired from waiting, and from being hungry and cold too, that she slumps over sideways a bit and leans her cheek against her right shoulder. The sun is shining in a thousand stars on the sea, opening that fiery path onto which you can slip and be off.

She's dreaming perhaps. There, at the end of the twinkling pathway, stands her mother, waiting for her, wearing her pale blue summer dress, and the light is shining on her black hair, on her bare shoulders. She is transfigured, buoyant, just as in the old days, when she would come back from the beach and the drops of seawater would roll slowly down the skin of her arms, shimmering. She's beautiful and happy, as though she need never die. It is especially to see her that Annah comes here, to her hiding place atop the escarpment. And then there's also the presence that surrounds her; it's the gaze of an old man whom she doesn't know but who dwells up here, in these ruins. It was he who had shown her the way, the very first time, to the arched window, from where you can see the whole stretch of the sea. He's from some other land; he's remote and serene, somewhat sad as well, and he invariably shows her the sea. Annah loves to feel the presence of his gaze up here, on her, and on everything around her – on the old cement walls, on the ruined terraces, on the hanging gardens overrun with couch grass and acanthuses.

Why do they want to destroy it all? When Annah told Peter that she would stay up there, in her house, even if it meant her death, he hadn't answered. So she'd made him give his word to never tell anyone where her hiding place was, even if they beat him, even if they burned the soles of his feet with a candle.

This is her place up here and no one else's. She's known every stone, every tuft of thyme, every bramble bush for so long now. In the beginning, she was frightened of Yondaland because it was a wild and deserted place and the old abandoned theater looked like a ghostly castle. Even Peter never came up here. He'd rather stay below, hidden in the fallen rocks to keep a lookout. It was Peter who had broken the news to Annah, when the wreckers had come for the first time. He had told her once, very quickly, and then he'd repeated it several times because the little girl didn't seem to understand; and then finally, she had felt a sudden, cold chill wash over her, and her head had begun to spin, as if she were going to faint. Afterward, she'd run all the way to Yondaland, and she'd seen the fences and the barbed wire, the signs, and the big yellow machines, stopped on the edge of the road way up there, like gigantic insects.

Suddenly, she hears explosions. They are tremendous blasts that shake the foundations of the stone escarpment, bringing dust down into her hair. At the end of the sweeping arm, the mass of cast iron swoops heavily and falls upon the walls of the old theater. Annah was expecting it, and yet she can't keep from crying out in fear. With all her strength, she clings to the ledge of the window, huddles against the wall. But the blows come, prolonged, far between, so intense that the little girl is bumped about and bruised. The sound of the first walls crumbling is terrifying. The stale smell of dust floats in the air; a gray cloud covers the sky and the sea; it is smothering the sun. Annah would like to cry out so that it will all stop, but she's paralyzed with fear, and the vibrations are jarring her out toward the precipice. The crashing sound of the tumbling walls is very near now. On the end of the giant arm the black ball wavers, falls, heaves back up, falls again. They're going to destroy everything, maybe the whole world – the rocks, the mountains – and then bury the sea and the sky under the rubble and the dust. Annah is lying on the window ledge, sobbing, waiting for the blow that will crush her, that will destroy the house that she loves.

The blows are coming more frequently, falling so near to her that she can taste the powder and the smell of sulfur in her lungs; she can see the sparks raining down around her. The heavy mass is pounding deep within her, blindly, relentlessly battering down the walls, bashing in the floorboards, twisting the creaking metal structures, moving steadily toward the stone wall that stands facing the sea and the sky.

Then, incomprehensibly, everything stops. A thick, anxiety-ridden silence settles back in. The dust drifts slowly down, as in the aftermath of an eruption. There are shouts, calls. The wreckers have gone down to the foot of the escarpment; they're looking up at the window. Annah knows now that it was Peter who betrayed her. He talked; he led them to her hiding place. And now, they're calling her, waiting for her. But she doesn't move.

There is a man in front of her; he's climbed up a ladder, and he's leaning on the window ledge, looking at her. "What are you doing up here?" He speaks very gently, holding out his hand to her. "Come on, you can't stay here." Annah shakes her head. The knot in her throat is so tight that she can't speak. The terrifying sound of destruction remains within her, and it seems as though she will never be able to speak again. The man leans forward; he picks the little girl up in his arms. He is very strong; his blue overalls are covered with dust and debris; his yellow helmet shines brightly in the sun.

Now Annah is feeling terribly tired; her eyes droop shut, as though she were going to fall asleep. When they get to the bottom of the ladder, the man sets her down on the ground. The workmen are there, motionless, not saying a word, their yellow helmets gleaming. Peter is standing next to them, and when she looks at him, he has an odd grin on his face, like a grimace, and in spite of her deep grief, Annah feels like laughing. She shrugs her shoulders and thinks: I'll just have to find something else.

Despite the hot sun and the dry dust, Annah is shivering with cold. The man with the yellow helmet wants to put a workman's jacket over her shoulders, but she pulls away and refuses. Among the men who are there, there's also someone in a brown suit that is too large for him, and Annah recognizes one of the supervisors from the school. Together, they start up toward the top of the cliff, where the blue police van is waiting by the highway.

Annah knows that she won't talk, that she won't say a word, ever. Walking up the path toward the police van, she turns slightly around and takes one last look at the stone wall and the sparkling sea. Yondaland is no more, it is a mere pile of ruins, the color of old dust. The old man's gaze is already drifting away, like the thin plumes of a dying fire. But the reflection of the sun on the sea shines upon the little girl's face and fills her dark eyes with a light that anger cannot dim.

David

S OMETIMES he thinks that the street belongs to him. It's the only place he really loves, especially at daybreak, when there's still no one around and the cars are cold. David wishes that things were always like that, with the bright sky over the dark houses and the silence, the vast silence that you'd think had come down from heaven to bring peace to earth. But do angels really exist? Long ago, his mother had told him long stories about angels with great wings of light, angels that floated around in the sky over the city and came down to help those in need, and she said that you knew when the angel was near when you felt a quick breeze on your neck, light as a breath, that made you shiver. His brother Edward used to make fun of him because he believed those stories, and he said there was no such thing as angels, that there were only airplanes in the sky. And what about clouds? But how did clouds prove that angels existed? David can't remember anymore, and no matter how hard he tries, nothing comes back to him.

But the morning, right now, is free – too free – because there's nothing left; no one is waiting anymore. And yet he wishes it would never end because afterward is terrifying. Afterward, when the day has really begun and the cars are driving on the streets, the cars, the buses, the motorcycles, and all the people are walking around with such hard faces. Where are they going? What do they want? David would rather think of angels, the ones that fly so high that they can't even see the earth any longer, just the white blanket of clouds slipping slowly under their wings. But it always has to be the morning sky, so vast and pure, because that's when the angels can probably float around for a long time without being in danger of running into airplanes.

At six o'clock in the morning, the street is calm and beautiful. As soon as he's closed the door to the apartment and put the string with the key hanging on it around his neck and zipped up his blue plastic jacket, David is off into the street. He runs between the stopped cars, goes up the flight of stairs, and stops in the center of the small square, his heart racing as if someone were following him. There's no one around, and dawn is barely beginning to break, fading the gray sky, but the houses are still dark, with shutters fastened tight, shut into their chilly morning sleep. There are pigeons already flapping up in front of David with a great flutter of wings. They fly up to the edges of the roofs, cooing. The rumbling of motors hasn't started yet, nor the voices of human beings.

Without intending to, David has walked up to the door of the school. It's an ugly gray cement building that nudged its way in between the old stone houses, and David stares at the door, painted in dark green, scarred at the bottom from children's shoes. But maybe he hasn't really come here accidentally; maybe he just wants to see it one more time – the door and the wall too, with its graffiti; the stairs covered with chewing gum; the old, dirty, wire-grated windows. He wants to look at it all again, and the thought that this will be the last time makes his heart beat faster, as if everything has already changed and he were being chased, pursued. It's the last time, the last time; that's what he's thinking, and the thought keeps going around in his head till it makes him dizzy. He didn't tell anyone, not even his mother, but now it's a sure thing; it's all over with.

Even so, he stays there for a long time, sitting on the short stairway leading up to the door, until the sound of the street cleaner pulls him from his daydream. The water gushes from the hose; making tearing noises and explosions, it streams down the narrow streets. The jet of water echoes on the metal bodies of the stopped cars, whisks trash along in the gutters. David gets up, turns away from the school, and starts to walk across town.

On the other side of the large avenue is the new part of town, mysterious, dangerous. He's already been there with his brother Edward;

he remembers it all – the stores, the tall buildings standing before their asphalt lots, the streetlamps taller than trees that by night cast their orangey, blinding light. Those are places no one goes; no one knows anything about them. Places you get lost in.

It's a big city, so big that you never see the end of it. Maybe you could walk for days and days along the same avenue, and night would come, and the sun would rise, and you'd still be walking along walls, crossing streets, parking lots, esplanades, and you'd still see the windshields and the headlights of the cars glimmering on the horizon like a mirage.

That's right: go away and never come back. David's heart sinks a little, because he can remember his brother Edward saying before he left, "One day I'll go away, and you'll never see me again." He wasn't bragging when he'd said that, but his eyes were so full of dark despair that David went to hide in the alcove to cry. It's always so awful to say things and then do them.

Today isn't just any old day. This is the first day that the summer sun has come to light up the facades of the houses, shine on the metal bodies of the cars. It's sparkling on everything, burning your eyes, and despite being afraid and full of doubt, David still feels happy that he's in the street. That's why he left the apartment so early, as soon as his mother had closed the door to go to work; he went out before even eating the piece of buttered bread she'd left on the table; he raced down the stairs and went running into the street with the key bouncing and thumping on his chest. That's why, and also because of his brother Edward, because he'd thought about him all night, at least a good part of the night, before he fell asleep.

"I'll go far away and I'll never come back." That's what his brother Edward had said, but he had waited for almost a year before doing it. His mother thought that he'd forgotten all about it, and everyone else – I mean everyone who had heard him say that – thought the same thing, but David hadn't forgotten. He thought about it every day and at night too, but he never said anything. Anyway, it would have been pointless to say, "When are you going away forever?" Because his brother Edward would undoubtedly have shrugged his shoulders and not answered. Maybe he didn't have the slightest idea back then.

It was a day like today, David remembers very well. Even the sun was up in the blue sky, and the streets in the old part of town were clean and empty, just like after a rain, because the street cleaner had just gone by. But it was very empty and very frightening, and the light that shone on the windows and the pigeons cooing and the voices of children that you could hear calling to one another from house to house in the labyrinth of still dark streets and even the calm, early morning silence were awful because David and his mother hadn't slept that night, waiting for him to come home, listening for his knock at the door, always the same knock: tap-tap-tap, tap-tap. Then since it was a Sunday and his mother wasn't going to work, the small apartment was filled with so much tension that David couldn't stand it, and he went out for the whole day, walking through the streets, going from house to house, looking for a sign, listening for a voice, all the way out to the public parks, all the way out to the beach. The seagulls flew up as he walked along the shore, coming to rest a little farther off, squawking because they don't like to be disturbed.

But David doesn't want to think about that day too much because he knows that the anxious feeling might come back. Then he thinks of his mother, sitting on the chair by the window, waiting, as motionless and heavy as a statue. He sits down on a bench in the small square, watching the people that are beginning to move around and the children running and shouting before school starts.

It's hard to be alone when you're small. David thinks about his brother Edward; he remembers him very clearly now, as if he'd left only day before yesterday. He was fourteen; he'd just turned fourteen when it happened, and David is barely nine now. That's too little to go away; maybe that's why his brother Edward hadn't wanted to take him along. Does a nine-year-old know how to run, how to fight, earn a living, how to keep from getting lost? Yet one day they'd had a fight in the apartment – what was it about? He can't remember, but they'd had a real fight, and before his brother got the better of him with an armlock around his neck, Edward fell down; David had made him fall with a leg trip, and his brother had said a little breathlessly, "You can fight pretty well for a small fry." David remembers that very well.

Where is he now? David thinks about it so hard that he can feel his heart pounding heavily in his chest. Is it possible that he doesn't hear it too, wherever he is, that he doesn't feel his eyes calling out to him? But maybe he's over at the other end of the city or even farther away, out beyond the boulevards and the avenues – like wide, unbridged moats – over on the other side of the white cliffs of the buildings, lost, alone. It's because of money that he left, because his mother didn't want to give him anything, because she took what he earned as an apprentice mechanic and he never had any money to go to the movies, to play football, to buy ice cream, or to play the pinball machines in the cafés.

Money is dirty; David hates it, and he hates his brother Edward for having left because of that. Money is ugly, and David scorns it. The other day, in front of his friend Hoceddine, David threw a coin into a hole in the sidewalk, just like that, for the fun of it. But Hoceddine said he was crazy, and he tried to fish the coin out with a twig but didn't succeed. When he has money one day, David thinks he'll throw it on the ground or into the sea so that no one will find it. He doesn't need anything. When he gets hungry in the streets, he prowls around the grocery stores and takes whatever he can – an apple or a tomato – then he quickly runs away through the narrow streets. Since he is small, he can fit into tons of hiding places – basement windows, cubbyholes under stairways, garbage sheds, behind doors. No one can catch him. He runs far away and eats the fruit slowly, without making a mess. He throws the peelings and the seeds in the gutter. He likes tomatoes best of all; that always surprised his brother Edward; in the old days, he'd even nicknamed him that – "Tomato" – but it wasn't mean at all; maybe down deep he even admired him for it; that was the only thing he couldn't do.

Oh yes, he really liked his name too, the name David. It was their father's name, before he died in a truck accident; his name was David Mathis, but he was so young that he can't even remember anymore. And their mother never wanted to talk about their father, except sometimes to say that he didn't leave her anything when he died, because then she'd had to go out and start working as a housemaid to feed her two children. But his brother Edward must remember him because he was six or seven when his father died, so maybe that was why his voice sounded funny sometimes and his eyes got bleary when he repeated his name: "David... David...."

As he walks down the large avenue, the sound of the cars and trucks is suddenly terrifying, unbearable. The sun is shining brightly in the sky, throwing bursts of light off the metal cars, lighting up the high fronts of the white buildings. There are people walking on the sidewalk here, but they aren't poor people like in the old part of town – Arabs, Jews, foreigners, dressed in old gray and blue clothes; they are people that David doesn't know, very tall, very strong. David is glad he's small because nobody seems to notice him; no one can see his bare feet stuck into the rubber shoes or his pants worn thin at the knees or, above all, his thin pale face, his dark eyes. For a second, he wants to turn back while there's still time, and his hand automatically clutches the key hanging around his neck.

But always, whenever he's afraid of something, he thinks of the story his mother used to tell him, the one about the young shepherd who killed a giant with a single stone thrown from his sling when all the soldiers and even the great king were terrified. David loves that story, and his brother Edward loves it too, and maybe that's why he repeated his name over and over like that, as if there was something supernatural in the syllables of the name. In the old days, he wouldn't have been afraid to walk here with him, down this endless street. But today, it's not the same because he knows that his brother Edward walked here before he disappeared. He knows it deep down inside, even better than if he saw his footprints on the cement sidewalk. He'd come this way and then disappeared forever. David would like to forget what that word "forever" means because it hurts him; it gnaws at his insides, at his stomach.

But you have to watch out for people, passersby, who walk along, walk blindly along. The sun is high in the cloudless sky; the white buildings are glittering. David has never seen so many people, all strangers, and shop windows, restaurants, cafés. His brother Edward came this way because it was money he wanted; he wanted to conquer money. In the dark streets, in the apartment, in the clammy, lightless corridors, poverty is like a wet sheet on your skin, or worse – like a damp, dirty skin you can't shed. But here, the light and the noise burn on your skin, burn your eyes; the rumbling of the motors rips your memories away. David is making a desperate effort not to forget it all; he wants to always remember it. His brother Edward told him that it was better to die in prison than to continue living there in the dark apartment. But when David had repeated that to his mother, she got angry, and she threatened to put him in a reform school very far away, for a long time. She said that he'd be a thief, a murderer, and even other things that David hadn't understood very well, but his brother Edward was terribly pale, and he listened, and there was a gleam in his dark eyes that David didn't like, and even today, when he remembers that, his heart starts racing as if he were afraid.

"Coward, yellowbelly, dirty rat, bastard"; that's what his brother Edward had said the next day, and he'd beaten him as hard as he could, even hitting him in the face with his fists until David started crying. So that's why he left, forever, because David had told his mother, had said that it was better to die in prison.

Then all of a sudden David starts feeling very tired. He looks back and sees the whole stretch of avenue he's walked down – the buildings, the automobiles, the trucks, all of it exactly the same as what lies before him. Where should he go? He finds a bus stop and sits down on the little plastic bench. On the ground there are used tickets that people have discarded. David picks one up, and when the bus comes, he waves it down and climbs inside and puts the unstamped end of the ticket into the punch. He goes to sit in the back of the bus; if a ticket collector gets on, it will be easier to get off before he reaches him. In the old days, his brother Edward used to take him to the stadium like that, on Sundays, and they bought chewing gum with the bus money. David preferred to buy a piece of warm bread in a bakery. But today he doesn't even have a coin in his pocket to buy bread. He thinks of the coin he threw into the hole in the sidewalk; maybe he should have tried to fish it out today?

The bus cruises along by the dry bed of the rio, where there are large grounds covered with cars standing still and barren vacant lots. Now there are long, high walls standing on the edge of the river, with thousands of windows, all identical, upon which the sun is shining as if it would never stop. Far, far away, but where is the city? Where is the sea, where are the dark narrow streets, the stairways, the roofs with the pigeons cooing? Here, it seems like there's never been anything else; never anything but these towering walls and esplanades and vacant lots where the grass doesn't grow.

When the bus reaches the end of the line, David starts walking down the avenue again, along the dry rio. Then he sees a flight of stairs, and he goes down to the riverbed, sits amid the piles of shingles; there are dead branches, broken crates, even an old mattress with rusty springs. David walks over the shingles through the debris, as if he were looking for something. It's nice here; you can hardly hear the cars and trucks except for the screeching of brakes from time to time or the long blaring of a horn that seems to bark out from beyond the high walls of buildings. It's a good place for rats and stray dogs, and David isn't afraid of them. All the same, he picks out a nice, smooth round stone on the beach, like the shepherd in the story he so loves, and he puts it in his pocket. With the stone, he feels safer.

He stays in the bed of the dry rio for a long time. This is the first place he feels comfortable, far from the city, far from the cars and trucks. Already the sunlight is less bright. A fine mist is beginning to slowly veil the sky. The buildings loom high on each side of the river, mountains of cement with tiny windows like snake holes. The sky is immense, and David thinks about the clouds that he used to love to watch, lying on his back in a park or on the stones of the beach. You could see the shapes of angels and the yellow sunlight reflected on the feathers of their wings. He never told anyone about that because you should never talk about angels to anyone.

Today, right now, maybe they'll come back because they really need to. David lies down in the riverbed, just like in the old days, and he stares at the dazzling sky through his squinting eyelids. He stares, waits; he wants to see something go by, someone, even just a bird so he can follow it with his eyes, try and take off with it. But the sky is completely empty, pale and bright, reaching its painful emptiness right down into his body.

It's been such a long time since David has felt that: like a whirlpool twisting up from deep within, pushing out all boundaries, as if you were a tiny gnat fluttering in front of a bright floodlight. Now David recalls the day he went looking for his brother Edward through all the

narrow streets, in the squares, deep in the dark courtyards, even calling out his name. It was Sunday; it was cold because it was still mid-
winter. The sky was gray and the wind was blowing. But the dizzy
anxiety was rising within him, almost until he could no longer con-
tain it in his body, and his heart was beating very fast because his
mother was waiting at home alone, sitting very still and cold on the
chair, with her eyes riveted on the door. He'd found him on the beach
with some other boys his age. They were sitting in a circle, protected
from prying eyes and the cold wind by the supporting wall of the
road. When David walked up, one of the boys – the youngest, whose
name was Corto – had turned around and said something; the other
boys hadn't moved, but his brother came over to him and said in a
cold voice, "What do you want?" And his eyes were strange, glassy, as
if he had a fever, scary. Since David didn't answer, he added in that
cruel stranger's voice, "Did she send you to spy on me? Get lost, go
home." Then Corto came up, and he was a peculiar boy who had a
girl's face and a long, thin body like a girl's but a very deep voice for
his age, and he said, "Leave him alone. Maybe he wants to play ball
with us?" His brother Edward just stood there, not moving, as if he
didn't understand. Then with an odd sort of smile, Corto said to
David, "Come on, kid; we're having a nice ballgame." So David automatically followed Corto over to the place where they were all sitting
on the stones in a circle, and he saw a closed tube of glue on a plastic
bag on the ground in the center of the circle, and there was also a
sheet of blotting paper folded in two that the boys were passing
around, taking turns putting their faces in the paper, breathing in,
closing their eyes, and coughing a little. Then Corto held out the
folded paper to David and said, "Go ahead, take a deep breath; you'll
see stars." And in the blotting paper there was a big gob of sticky glue,
and when David sniffed it, the smell went straight through him, all of
a sudden, and made his head spin, and he started trembling and then

crying because of all the emptiness out there on the beach by the dirty wall with Edward, who hadn't come home since morning.

Then something strange happened; David remembers it perfectly well. His brother Edward put his arm around him and helped him get up and walk along the beach, and he went back to the apartment, and his mother hadn't dared say anything to him or even yell, even though he'd been out all day and hadn't even come home for lunch, but Edward led him over to the alcove and helped him get to bed, and afterward he went to bed himself. But it wasn't to go to sleep because David saw his open eyes watching him right up to the moment he sank into sleep.

Now it's just like that: the whirlpool is coming back, creating a void in his body and head, and blackness is rushing in just as if you were falling into a deep well. It's the silence and the loneliness that are causing it. David looks around: the stretch of dusty shingles, the rubbish strewn about in the riverbed, and he feels the silence bearing down on him. The sky is very bright, a little yellow because the sun is setting. Nobody comes out here, nobody, ever. It's only a place for rats and those flat flies that look for food in the garbage that people leave in the riverbed.

David is hungry too. He remembers he hasn't eaten anything since last night or drunk anything either. He's hungry and thirsty, but he doesn't want to go back to the old part of town. He walks along the shingle beach till he comes to the slow, winding stream of water. The water is cold and clear, and he takes a long drink, kneeling on the shingles with his face right down near the water. Having drunk like that makes him feel a little better, and he feels strong enough to walk back up the riverbed to an access ramp further upstream. That is where the trucks come to dump their loads of stones, debris, mud.

David leaves the banks of the dry rio, goes back in among the houses to find something to eat. The white buildings make a sort of

semicircle around a large lot filled with stopped cars. At the far end of
the lot there is a shopping center with a wide, dark door. The lights are
already shining around the door to make people think that night has
come.

David really likes the night. He isn't afraid of it; on the contrary, he
knows he can hide when it falls; it's as if he becomes invisible. In the
supermarket there are lots of lights. The people come and go with
their little metal carts. David knows what he needs to do. His friend
Lucas showed him how the first time. You have to pick out some
people to go in with, choose people that look respectable, maybe with
a young child. Grandparents are the best, pushing a cart with a baby
in it. They walk slowly and don't pay attention to things around them,
so you can go in with them and pretend like you're with them, sometimes up in front, sometimes lagging behind. The floorwalkers don't
watch grandparents with children.

David waits for a little while in a corner of the parking lot. He sees
a big, black car stop and a man and a woman who are still young get
out, along with their whole family – five children. There are three girls
and two boys; the girls are tall and pretty, with long, dark blond hair
that tumbles down in cascades on their shoulders, except for the
littlest one, who's four or five years old and has dark hair. The two
boys are somewhere between eleven and fifteen; they look like their
father; they're tall and thin with tanned skin and they have light
brown hair. They all walk toward the door of the Supermarket. The
little girl is put into a metal cart, and an older girl pushes her, laughing
loudly. The mother calls her; she shouts their names: "Christiane!
Isa!" And the boys run after them and stop the cart.

David follows them, first from a distance, then he goes into the Supermarket with them. He's so close that he can hear them talking; he
listens to everything they are saying. The children separate into
groups of two, join together again, run off, come back; they even

swarm around David, but without seeing him, as if he were no more than a shadow. They lure their parents over to the bakery section, and David takes the opportunity to grab a loaf of bread, which he eats leisurely, slice after slice. The girls are pretty, and David stares at them so intently it is almost painful. The electric light shines on their blond hair, on their blue or red plastic parkas. The eldest girl is named Sonia; she must be sixteen years old, and it is her that David stares at most of all. She is so sure of herself; she speaks so easily in that lilting voice of hers, pushing back the strands of hair that fall on her cheeks, that brush up against her lips. David thinks of his brother Edward, of his dark, hardened face, of his black eyes burning feverishly. He thinks of Corto too, on the beach, of his pale complexion, his troubling eyes with the brown circles that mar his face; he thinks of the cold wind on the deserted beach. The children are milling around him, shouting, laughing, calling each other. David listens avidly to their names ringing out: "Alan! Isa! Dino! Sonia! . . ." At one point, the parents turn around and look in astonishment at David eating the slices of bread, as if they were going to say something to him. But David turns away; he stops and lets them walk off, then he starts following them again, but from a distance. As he goes by the shelves of snack food, he chooses a package of cheese crackers and starts munching on them. But they're too salty and make him thirsty. So he puts down the opened package and takes a box of fig bars that he really likes. The family in front of him is piling a lot of things into the cart – cookies, bottled water, milk, sacks of potatoes, packages of pasta, soap. The cart is so heavy that the boys are pushing it now, and the little girl is sucking her thumb and looking bored.

David thinks that he wants to follow them like that all his life, to the very ends of the earth, all the way to their house. In the evenings, they'd all go into a beautiful, well-lit house surrounded by a cool garden filled with flowers and willows, and they'd all eat around a large table like the ones you see in the movies, and there would be all sorts of dishes and fruits and bowls full of ice cream. And their parents would talk with them and tell them all stories, long stories that would make them burst out laughing, and then it would be time to go to bed – first of all little Christiane, and they would tell her a bedtime story; everyone would have their turn, until their eyes drooped shut; then they'd go and lie down in their beds; everyone would have their own bed, fitted with patterned sheets like you see sometimes, and the room would be very big and painted in pale blue. And before she went to bed, Sonia would come in her nightgown, with her long blond hair that ripples over her shoulders, and she would give him a little kiss with puckered lips, and he'd breathe in the warmth of her neck and the fragrance of her hair just before dropping off to sleep. That's exactly how it would be; David can see it when he closes his eyes.

Now they are all walking by the fruit stand, and they stop to pick some out. David wants so much to hear their voices again and be enveloped in their fragrance that he comes back to his senses, standing there in their midst. He stops just beside Sonia; for her, he chooses a nice red apple, and holds it out to her. She looks at him a little surprised, and then she flashes him a kind smile but doesn't take the apple. The family walks away again, and David eats the apple slowly as tears blur his eyes a bit, though he doesn't understand why he feels like crying. He watches as they walk away to the other end of the big store, turn behind a mountain of beer bottles. Then, without even trying to escape notice, he walks out of the Supermarket, passing between the cash registers, and goes to finish his apple outside and look at the darkness that has settled over the parking lot.

He stays there for a long time, sitting on a cement curb near the exit to the parking lot, watching the cars switch on their headlights and drive away. One after the other, they slam their doors and then slip away into the distance, disappear, along with their taillights and their blinking signals. Despite the chill of the night, David loves to see the automobiles drive away like that, with reflections on their shiny bodies and their headlights on. But you have to watch out for policemen and guards. They have black cars, sometimes mopeds, and they drive slowly around the parking lots looking for thieves. All of a sudden, David notices that someone is looking at him. It's a tall, hefty man with a brutal face who came out of the Supermarket through a side door and walked silently over the pavement behind David. Now he's there, looking at him, and his eyes are gleaming oddly in the light from the front of the Supermarket. But he's not a guard or a policeman. He's holding a bag of popcorn in his hand, and now and again he pushes his hand up against his mouth to swallow the popcorn without taking his dark, very shiny eyes from David. David glances over at him every few seconds and sees him coming nearer; he hears the sound that the thick hand makes as it rummages in the bag of popcorn. He's very near now, and David's heart starts pounding very hard because he remembers the things they say at school – crazy, perverted men that kidnap children and kill them. At the same time, he is so petrified with fear that he can't budge from the place he is sitting on the cement curb, looking straight out over the almost empty parking lot with the large yellow patches of light from the streetlamps.

"Do you want some popcorn?" When David hears the man's voice – he spoke very softly but with a slight quavering sound, as if he too were afraid – he leaps up from the curb and starts running as fast as he can toward the entrance of the parking lot where some cars are still parked. As soon as he passes the first car, he stops, lies flat on the ground, and crawls under the vehicles, going from one to the other; then he stops again and looks around. The man is there; he'd run after him, but he is too fat to get down on his hands and knees; he is striding along next to the cars. David sees his feet go past, walk away. He waits a little longer and then starts crawling in the opposite direction.

When he comes out from under a parked truck, he sees the silhouette of the man off in the distance, walking away and looking over his shoulder.

David is not so frightened anymore, but he doesn't dare wander around in the night anymore. The bed of the truck is covered with a tarpaulin, and David unties one side and slips under the tarp. The metal floor is cold, covered with cement dust. Up near the cab, David finds some old pieces of canvas, and he makes a bed from them. Hunger, fear, and spending the whole day walking outside have tired him out. He lies down on the canvases and goes to sleep listening to the sound of cars passing on the road running along the dry rio. Maybe he thinks of his brother Edward one more time, alone in the night, just as he is.

When day breaks, David awakens before it is even light. His body aches from the cold night and the hard floor in the bed of the truck. The wind whips at the tarpaulin, lifting it up and slapping it back down, letting in gusts of cold, damp air and the gray light of dawn.

David climbs down from the truck, walks across the parking lot. The wide road is deserted, still lit by the yellow pools of the streetlamps. But David really loves this hour of the day, so early in the morning that all the inhabitants of the city seem to have fled far into the hills. Maybe they'll never come back either?

He strolls across the road and walks along the quay. Down below, the dry rio is vast and silent. The bed of shingles stretches as far as you can see upstream and downstream. In the middle, the thin current of water flows relentlessly on, still dark, the color of night. David goes down the access ramp to the river; he walks over the shingles. It seems as if the sound of his footsteps must be waking up the sleeping creatures, the large flat flies, horseflies, rats. When he is near the water, he squats down on his heels, watches the stream rushing past, spinning into whirlpools, digging out hollows.

Slowly, the day filters in; the gray shingles begin to glitter; the water becomes lighter, transparent. There is a kind of mist rising from the riverbed, and now David can no longer see the banks or the streetlamps or the ugly houses with closed windows. He shudders and brushes his hand against the water, scoops some up with his fingers. He doesn't know why, but all of a sudden he thinks of his mother, who must be waiting for him in the dark apartment, sitting on a chair, watching the door. He'd like to go back with his brother Edward; now he knows that is the reason he left, and he knows he won't find him. He'd tried not to think of that so it wouldn't ruin his chances, but he'd thought that luck would guide him through all the streets, the boulevards, among all the people who know where they are going, to the lost place. He hadn't found anything; there's no such thing as luck. Even if he searched for a hundred years, he couldn't find him. He knows that now; he's not desperate, but it's as if something has changed deep down inside of him, and he will never be the same again.

So he watches the light spreading slowly over the riverbed. The sky is clear and cold; the light is cold too, but it makes David feel better; it gives him strength. The mist of dawn has cleared. Now you can see the giant buildings on either side of the river again. The sun shines white on their facades to the east, glints off the huge windows with no one behind them.

When David gets hungry, he goes back toward the Supermarket. There's nobody around yet at this hour, and the nasal music from the loudspeakers seems to echo from the depths of a huge, empty cave. Inside the store, the neon light is harsh and steady; it makes colors and objects stand out brightly. David isn't hiding anymore. There are no families or children he can latch onto. Only busy people – employees in white coats, cashiers behind their cash registers. David eats some fruit, standing in front of the display – a yellow apple, a banana, some purple grapes. Nobody pays any attention to him. He feels very small, almost invisible. But at one point, a young girl wearing the store's white coat looks at him eating, and there is a strange smile on her face, as if she recognizes him. But she continues putting items on the food shelves without saying anything.

Just as he is going out of the Supermarket, David gets the urge to take the money. It comes over him all of a sudden, just like that; maybe it was the long hours of waiting; maybe it was the night or the loneliness on the shingles of the dry rio. Suddenly David understands why his brother Edward never came back, why he couldn't be found. It happens in front of the shoe store. David remembers the day when he and his mother went to the police station and waited for a long, long time before going into the inspector's office. His mother wasn't saying anything, but the man was asking questions in a soft voice, and every now and again he looked at David straight in the eye, and David tried to hold his gaze with his heart pounding wildly. Maybe his mother knew something, something terrible that she didn't want to say, something that had happened to his brother Edward. She was so pale and silent, and the man who was sitting behind the metal table had eyes that shone like jade, and he tried to find out; he asked questions in his soft voice.

That's why David has stopped in front of the large shoe store, where the white light is shining on the red plastic tiles. He does it almost automatically, as though he were repeating the motions of someone who had come before him. Slowly, he walks down the aisles that lead toward the other end of the store. He goes past rows of shoes without seeing them, but he can smell the sharp odor of leather and plastic. A light that makes his head swim is reflecting from the red tiles; the sugary music floating down from the ceiling is a little nauseating. There's no one in the big store. The employees are standing by the door, talking, not looking at the young boy walking toward the other end of the store.

The voices coming from the soft music are covering everything else, going:

Ah ooh, ahwa, wahahoo . . .

like birds calling in the forest. But David doesn't pay any attention to what they're saying; he keeps walking, holding his breath, toward the other end of the store, where the cash register is. Nobody sees him; nobody thinks about him. He walks noiselessly through the aisles of shoes, boots, tennis shoes, baby booties, toward the cash register, holding the round stone he found last night on the riverbank tightly in his hand. His heart is pounding hard in his chest, so hard that he thinks it must be echoing through the whole store. The light from the neon tubes is blinding; bright, steady gleams of light shoot from the mirrors on the walls and pillars. The red plastic floor is immense and barren; David's feet are slipping over it as if it were ice. He thinks of the guards that go around in stores and in parking lots in their gray cars; he thinks of the mean people watching with shiny, ruthless eyes. His heart races, races, and sweat moistens his brow, the palms of his hands. Over there, at the other end of the store, huge and brightly lit in the neon lamps, he can clearly see the cash register, standing very still; he goes toward it, toward the place where he will finally be able to find out, finally be able to meet his brother Edward, the burning place where the secret message is hidden. Now he understands it; he's found it; that's why he left the apartment yesterday morning with the key tied around his neck: to get here, get to the place where he can start finding his brother again. He moves toward the cash register as if it were actually hiding his brother, as if when he drew near, he would see his thin, dark silhouette appear, his handsome face with the black eyes burning feverishly, his tousled, curly hair as if he'd been walking in the wind.

He is gripping the round stone very tightly. The stone is very warm and damp from the sweat in his hand. This is how you make war with giants, all alone in the vast, deserted valley, filled with blinding light. You can hear the cries of wild animals in the distance – wolves, hyenas, jackals. They are whining in the silent wind. And the voice of the giant rings out; he laughs, and he shouts at the child walking toward him, "Come forward; I'll make food for the birds in the sky and the creatures of the field out of you. Come forward!! . . ." And his laughter makes shivers run through the round stone from the riverbed.

Now David is at the back of the large store where the cash register stands. The white light from the ceiling is reflecting off its metallic corners, off the black plastic of the counter, off the blood red floor. David isn't looking at anything but the cash register; he moves toward it, touches it with his fingertips; he goes around the counter to get closer still. The soft music continues its distant sighing, its crooning, and the sound of David's heart thumping mingles with the slow notes of the music. It is a strange kind of dizziness, just like the kind that filled his head when he breathed into the blotting paper permeated with the peppery smell of glue. Maybe his brother Edward's face is there right now, beside him, dark and hieratic like the face of an Indian with high cheekbones, waiting. Who is holding him prisoner? Who keeps him from coming back? But the blinding emptiness whirls about him, and he can't understand.

David is leaning against the counter; his face is level with the cash register drawer. The drawer just happens to be open, and it slips slowly outward as if someone else's hand were opening it, taking the stack of bills, and closing a tight fist over it, crumpling it between the fingers.

But suddenly the emptiness stops, and only fear remains. Someone is there next to David – a young, slightly chubby man with an almost effeminate face framed with brown curly hair. He is holding David's fist, gripping it so fiercely between his two hands that David can hear his knuckles cracking and cries out in pain. The adolescent's face is glistening with sweat, and there is a cruel gleam in his eyes as he repeats through clenched teeth with so much vehemence he is spluttering, "Thief! Thief! Thief!" David doesn't say anything; he doesn't even struggle. His left hand has dropped the round stone from the river to the floor; it rolls over the red plastic and stops. "Thief! Dirty Thief!" repeats the young man tirelessly, and now he raises his voice to attract the attention of the salesgirls at the front of the store.

"Thief! Thief! Dirty little thief!" he shouts, and there is such a flustered and angry expression on his face that David isn't afraid of him anymore. He just closes his eyes and tries to fight the pain of the boy's two hands crushing his wrist and the bones in his fingers. He doesn't want to cry out or say anything because that's what he must do if he wants to find his brother Edward. The strangled voice of the young man rings in his ears, threatening and hateful: "Dirty thief! Dirty little thief!" But he mustn't answer, mustn't beg or cry or say that it wasn't he that came here, that it wasn't the money he wanted, but his brother Edward's face. He mustn't even think about that anymore because the giant has conquered him, and he won't be king and he won't find what he's looking for. But he mustn't say a thing, never a thing, even when the guards and the policemen come to take him to prison. Some women have come over now; they're standing around the two boys, talking, telephoning. One of them says, "Look, he's only a child, let him go." "And what if he runs away? He's a dirty little thief, like you see so many of around here; they wait for you to turn your back, and then they steal from the cash register." "What's your name? How old are you?" "It's their parents that train them to do it, you know; they have to bring money home every evening." "Thief, you dirty little thief!"

Finally the young man releases his hold, not so much out of pity but because his arms are tired from having squeezed David's hand so long. Then David falls onto the blood red floor; he crumples slowly, like a pile of rags, and his bruised hand and wrist hang limply by his side. The burning pain shoots all the way up under his shoulder, but he doesn't say anything, not a word, though salty tears run down his cheeks and wet the corners of his mouth.

Now silence sets in again for a few more minutes. No one is saying anything, and the young man has moved a few steps away from the cash register, as if her were afraid or ashamed. David still hears the languorous sounds of the far-off music, like the whimpering of restless animals; he hears his heart thumping loudly in his temples, in his neck, in the arteries at the crook of his elbow. The burning pain in his hand has subsided; he feels the wrinkled paper of the bills between his fingers that no one thought to take away from him. He struggles to lift himself up a little and heaves the wad of bills, which bounces across the linoleum like an old spitball. No one moves to pick them up. Before him, through the blur of his tears, he also sees the face of his mother, who is waiting in the dark apartment, far beyond the steep walls and the turbulent valleys of the modern city. He sees it in a flash, at the same time as the uniformed guards appear at the other end of the store. But it's all the same to him; he's not afraid of loneliness anymore, he can't fear the world any longer, nor the looks people give him, because now he's found the door that leads to his brother Edward, to his secret hiding place, the one you never come back from.

LaVergne, TN USA
03 November 2009

162937LV00001B/160/P